Dedicated to my daughter Stephanie,
with love.

Contents

1. Claire
2. St Luke's Hospital
3. Bank Nursing
4. Daphne
5. The Main Entrance
6. Matron Bain
7. Len
8. The Grand Summer Fete
9. Michael
10. Sid Sullivan
11. Brian
12. James (Jimmy) Murphy
13. My Diary
14. Ruby
15. Ada
16. The Staff Mugs
17. Selina
18. Bonfire Night
19. Valium The Ward Cat
20. Not All Carers Care
21. The ECT Suite
22. AWOL The Search
23. The Outing
24. The Fyshe
25. Nightingale House & Cavell House
26. Community Psychiatric Team
27. New Day – The Day Hospital
28. Additional Notes

About the Author

Michelle Karen is a retired mental health nurse and cognitive behavioural psychotherapist. She left her home in Guernsey for the south of England in 1983 to undertake registered mental health nurse training.

At a time when mental health was seldom discussed and widely misunderstood, pursuing this career was a challenging choice.

For over forty years, she worked in diverse settings, including adolescent care, prisons, acute wards, elderly care, and day centres. Her extensive experience provides a wealth of stories and insights that are harrowing, humorous, and deeply human.

Prologue

Are the Nurses Alright? offers a compelling account of the decline of psychiatric workhouses and the evolution of mental health care in England in the late 1980's.

It is an anecdotal account of mental health nursing, including entries from Claire's personal diary and additional clinical notes.

Set in a large, red-brick Victorian psychiatric hospital in England, at a time of fundamental change in the philosophy and practice of mental health provision, it shows the transition from institutional to community care in the 1980s and 1990s.

The hospital, village, characters, events, and dialogues portrayed are fictional. The stories are informed by real-life events, clinical observations, and nursing experiences. Any resemblance to actual persons, living or dead, is purely coincidental.

The title poses a question: *Are the nurses alright?* Reflecting a genuine concern for the well-being of those who selflessly devote themselves to caring for others.

The truth is, nurses remain unwavering in their commitment, tirelessly attending to patients with steadfast dedication. Their resilience is evident as they work, often without complaint, their uniforms blending them into a collective entity, each seemingly reduced to a mere number in the system. They are the unsung heroes, the backbone of the hospital.

Beneath their uniformity lies profound humanity. Each nurse carries their own burdens, challenges and uncertainties. Do they receive the recognition and support they deserve for their tireless efforts? Is their dedication truly valued? Does anyone genuinely stop to wonder, *Are the nurses alright?*

1
CLAIRE

"It does not matter how slowly you go, so long as you do not stop."
Confucius

Beep... beep... beep... beep... beep...

The shrill beeping of the alarm clock pierced the morning silence, rousing Claire from her slumber. With reluctant resolve, she opened one eye, squinting at the glowing digits of the clock before coaxing the other eye open. Yawning deeply, she stretched her limbs, the weariness of sleep still clinging to her frame. With a resigned sigh, she muttered sleepily to herself,

"Here we go, another day, another dollar."

Her hand moved with deliberate slowness to silence the persistent beeping, punctuating the dawn with a decisive jab. Thus began another day in Claire's world—a familiar rhythm of routine and responsibility awaiting her.

This morning, she was glad to be alone. Her body felt weighed down by fatigue. Her legs and back throbbed with a dull ache, and her eyelids clung stubbornly to the gritty remnants of sleep. She rubbed her eyes and mustered the strength to hoist herself out of bed, each movement a battle against the heaviness enveloping her. She shuffled towards the bathroom, navigating the familiar path with bleary-eyed determination.

She peered into the mirror, giving herself a wry smile. Despite it being only 5:45 am, Claire already felt as though she had completed a day's worth of toil. "Hey-ho, here we go..." she muttered, bracing herself for the demands of another day.

Making her way back to the bedroom, she picked up her leopard-print fleece dressing gown and the black socks she had worn the day before from the floor by her bed. She pulled them on, then padded downstairs.

The house was cold.

As she filled the kettle, her gaze fell upon the disheartening sight of the sink overflowing with dishes, some had a stubborn layer of fried egg and cold bacon grease that had solidified like wax. The sight seemed to mirror her own weariness. Sighing heavily, she felt the weight of exhaustion on her shoulders.

Her attempts to upcycle furniture into the shabby-chic style she admired in magazines had fallen short of the envisioned elegance, leaving the space feeling more shabby than chic. The downstairs rooms bore witness to half-finished projects and a kaleidoscope of clashing colours and patterns.

Despite the chaos, it was home to Claire Taylor and her children, Tom and Lizzie. Surveying her surroundings with a mixture of affection and resignation, she couldn't help but acknowledge the tired yet homely atmosphere. Amidst the clutter and weariness, there was a sense of belonging and acceptance that made it all worthwhile.

"Crikey, it's cold," she whispered through clenched teeth and shivered.

Plunging herself into the task at hand, she oscillated between sips of hot tea and scrubbing away at the remnants of last night's dinner. A sharp chill permeated the air, prompting further curses under her breath, her body instinctively recoiling against the cold.

Undeterred, she pressed on, tidying the kitchen and lounge swiftly, gathering and sorting magazines, books, blankets, and stray shoes into their designated places. Discarded cotton buds and cotton wool, stained with remnants of 'Pink Fizz' nail varnish, met their fate in the bin as she buzzed around. Satisfied with the semblance of order, she headed back upstairs, her thoughts already drifting towards the warmth of a soothing shower.

The house was quiet.

Claire and her husband Joe had separated a couple of years ago. They had grown apart over the fifteen years they had been married, and Joe's brief fling with one of his office co-workers had been the final straw. His impulsive and drunken confession about his infidelity one night prompted them to finally separate, rather than limping on miserably together 'for the sake of the children'.

Although it was painful at the time, they both agreed they were better and happier apart, which allowed them to separate and retain some respect for each other.

They managed, for the most part, to agree on a shared residence rota where the children stayed with each parent fifty percent of the time. This generally worked pretty well. There was a bit of bickering to start with, but over the months, things had settled down to a polite and civilised rhythm between them, the children, and their homes.

Tom and Lizzie seemed happy enough with the arrangement and had their own bedrooms in each house. Both sets of grandparents were still involved and supportive. There had been none of the drama, backstabbing, or bitter rhetoric that Claire and Joe had seen with the breakups of their friends and family.

Initially, Joe wanted to continue having regular meals as a family, wanting to foster a sense of continuity and connection despite the dissolution of their relationship. But Claire soon realised that she wanted a clean break, a chance to rediscover herself and chart her own path as a single mother.

The prospect of forging a new relationship held little appeal; what she craved most was the space to find her footing, to inhale deeply and begin again.

During the upheaval of their separation, Claire consoled herself with solitude, recognising the importance of self-discovery and personal growth as she navigated the rocky and uncharted waters of single parenthood. In the quiet expanse of her newfound independence, she embraced the opportunity to redefine herself and to carve out a future that resonated with her hopes.

Despite their shared history of fifteen years and two children, Claire and Joe's relationship had transformed into something akin to distant acquaintances. Their connection had simply fizzled out, leaving behind an atmosphere of cool detachment. Reflecting on their journey, she acknowledged that their union had never been a fiery or passionate romance, even at the beginning. Instead, it unfolded with a subdued rhythm, lacking the intensity and passion of enduring love stories. They met, had a short romance, and somehow drifted comfortably along together, ending up married with a house and two children because that's what everyone did. It wasn't unpleasant. It wasn't terrible. It just wasn't anything much at all.

In accepting this reality, Claire welcomed the quiet evolution of their new relationship and the value of mutual respect and understanding from their shared history.

When they first married, they had bought a doer-upper 'with potential'. A mid-terrace 1930s three-bedroom house, constructed with sturdy brickwork, and a façade accented by bay windows that welcomed natural light into the interior spaces. The blue front door opened into an entrance hall, leading to a cosy living room complete with tiled fireplace. The adjacent dining room was perfect for family gatherings, while the small kitchen, nestled at the rear, offered a practical space for cooking. Upstairs were three bedrooms, each with original built-in wardrobes and period details. A modest family bathroom completed the upstairs. The small, manageable garden reflected the functional house design and ethos of the time. The house immediately 'felt' right to Claire when they viewed it. It had history and felt lived in. In her mind's eye, she imagined how it could be renovated into a lovely family home. There was an initial excited flurry of activity when they moved in—stripping decades and layers of wallpaper, painting, and decorating.

Like their relationship, the excitement soon faded, and jobs were left undone, half-finished, or neglected.

When they decided to separate, the children quickly accepted their parents' decision and settled into their new living arrangements surprisingly easily. Claire was going to stay in the family home with the children and grateful for the familiar surroundings. The house offered comfort amid uncertainty for her and the children.

Meanwhile, Joe settled into his new home, a small, rented house a few streets away. Claire and Joe were good parents. They functioned better apart.

Their arrangement worked. Claire shouldered the responsibility of the mortgage, ensuring the stability of their shared assets, while Joe contributed his share through rent payments and contributions to expenses. Together, they worked out the intricacies of co-parenting, taking turns to attend school events, shuttle the children to their activities, and provide support through life's ebbs and flows. Though their paths diverged, their commitment to their children remained unwavering.

Claire was proud of the way they had made sensible decisions together and put their children's welfare above everything else. The arrangement was fair.

It was tough being a single parent, and she sometimes found herself longing for Joe during moments of sickness, loneliness, or fatigue. Yet, on reflection, she questioned whether it was Joe she missed or just the idea of having another adult to share the decision-making with. In her mind, at these times, he represented an idealised figure of stability and reliability.

With the hustle and bustle of her daily life—juggling work, caring for her children, maintaining the household and garden, nurturing a semblance of a social life, and striving to make ends meet—Claire seldom had the luxury to dwell on such thoughts. She tried to remain steadfast in her responsibilities, navigating the complexities of her life with determination and resilience, even though the memory of Joe lingered in her thoughts from time to time.

Getting back together was never going to be an option.

Matron Barbara Jones was her mum's best friend. She had spotted Claire's potential for a career in nursing and had taken her under her wing, encouraging her to pursue Registered Mental Health Nurse training. It was because of her encouragement that Claire decided to embark on a three-year journey toward becoming a registered nurse at St Luke's School of Nursing.

Claire was eternally grateful for all the support she'd had from Barbara and was delighted to receive letters and cards from her now she was retired and living happily in Spain, where she worked as a volunteer in a dog rescue centre.

Barbara always remembered the children at Christmas and birthdays. The letters enclosed with the cards were written in her old-fashioned loopy handwriting, filled with funny stories about living in Spain and her work with the dogs, puppies, and Spanish people. Having dedicated her life to caring for people, she now focused on dogs. She had never married or had children, describing herself always as 'happily single' and preferring the company and loyalty of dogs to people. Her letters described the dogs and the rescue centre work in such vivid detail that Claire felt as if she had visited it herself.

The nurse training curriculum at St Luke's was designed to bridge the gap between theory and practice, immersing students in a dynamic learning environment that mirrored the realities of healthcare. In between clinical placements, Claire and her classmates engaged in intensive study sessions, attended lectures, and underwent assessments that challenged their intellect and resolve.

Each cohort of nursing students was bestowed with an initial. For Claire and her fourteen fellow classmates, their initial was 'S'. Under the banner of 'S Group', they embarked on a voyage of discovery. It was a journey marked by laughter and tears, triumphs, and setbacks, but above all, a shared commitment to the noble calling of nursing.

Training began with a theoretical six-week classroom induction block, covering the foundational principles of nursing practice. From the intricacies of patient care to the complexities of medical ethics, Claire absorbed knowledge eagerly. The breadth of their education encompassed a diverse array of topics, spanning mental health, psychiatric disorders, and therapeutic interventions—from psychology to pharmacology, from counselling techniques to crisis intervention.

However, it was the clinical placements that truly defined S Group's journey. From the sterile corridors of the general hospital placements, the wards of psychiatric hospitals, and the bustling energy of community mental health centres, they ventured forth, learning on the job. In the chaos of their clinical rotations and study blocks, bonds were forged from their shared experiences. Even when their careers progressed and the years unfolded, the memories of their time at St Luke's remained. Some members of S Group developed enduring friendships that would last a lifetime.

I'm Claire

I'm Claire, a single mum and staff nurse. You already know a bit about me and my family, so welcome to my world.

The following stories, snapshots, and accounts are taken from the time towards the end of my nurse training and a couple of years working as a staff nurse on the bank at St Luke's Hospital. This was in the late 1980s and early 1990's when large institutions like St Luke's were closing due to financial constraints and there was a shift towards care in the community.

I've included some excerpts from my diary and added more detail in the additional notes (*).

I qualified as a Registered Mental Health Nurse (RMN) in 1987. (*1)

2
ST. LUKE'S HOSPITAL

"...the very first requirement in a hospital is that it should do the sick no harm."
Florence Nightingale, Notes on Hospitals (1863)

A typical Victorian asylum (*2), St Luke's, like many other psychiatric hospitals of its time, was a large, red-brick institutional building with vast surrounding grounds and gardens designed to provide a safe and secure environment for four hundred and fifty inpatients. Located on the outskirts of our village, St Luke's had a significant impact on the local community, both socially and economically. Over eighty percent of those living in the village were employed by the hospital.

I'd grown up with it. I loved the wide, tree-lined driveway, the buildings, and the huge hospital grounds.

The hospital was designed with a functional and practical approach, focusing on creating a calm and neutral environment that could help patients feel safe and secure. However, this approach also isolated patients from society, friends, and families, promoting stigma and institutionalisation. Naughty children were threatened with being sent to the 'nuthouse' or 'Loony Lukes'. They were warned that they would be locked away, never to be seen again if they didn't behave.

The interior was designed with patient safety in mind, with reinforced doors, secure windows, and restricted access to certain areas of the building. The wards, offices, waiting rooms, communal patient areas, cafés, social spaces, day centres, occupational therapy, art therapy, and industrial therapy departments were all linked by a maze of wide echoing corridors with shiny linoleum flooring. The beige corridor walls were painted half-height with dark blue gloss paint.

The corridors of St Luke's smelt like a mix of boiled vegetable soup, cooking oil, sweat, urine, and disinfectant. In my experience, all psychiatric hospitals have the same, highly memorable smell. My Uncle Tim, who worked as a hospital maintenance man, often joked that if he were blindfolded and taken to a mystery location, he would be able to tell it was a psychiatric hospital just by its smell. Once smelt, never forgotten.

The wards were named after flowers or trees. Not very original, but it made them easy to remember: Bluebell, Bay, Birch, Lavender, Linden, Larch, Maple, Myrtle, and Marigold, spanning a diverse spectrum of care specialties.

There were units dedicated to elderly care, offering compassionate support with services tailored to promote comfort and end-of-life care. Others catered for acute conditions, providing swift intervention and comprehensive medical care. The long-stay and rehabilitation wards focused on fostering recovery and independence. Some wards were secured with locked doors, where patients required permission or escorted time-out to navigate the outside world.

The delineation of single-sex wards, designated for either male or female patients, maintained a sense of privacy and dignity in the provision of care, while mixed-sex wards offered an environment of inclusivity and collaboration, fostering connections and camaraderie among patients from diverse backgrounds and experiences. Each ward played a vital role in the collective endeavour to restore health, dignity, and hope to those entrusted to its care.

Patients ranged in age from eighteen upwards, reflecting the diverse spectrum of mental health needs and life stages within the community. Among them, the hospital cared for individuals like Ethel, the oldest patient at ninety-eight. Her frail form bore the weight of time, her body wasted and thin, her once-nimble limbs now contracted and bent inward. Dementia had enveloped her mind, leaving her eyes vacant and unseeing, disconnected from the world around her. Lost in her own thoughts, she existed in a state of perpetual confusion, unaware of the passing days or the faces that tended to her needs. Bereft of visitors, she hopefully found comfort in the compassionate care provided by the ward staff, who tended to her with warmth and dedication.

Each day unfolded in a limbo of uncertainty until the inevitable moment when her weary heart would cease its rhythmic dance. Finally, her name found its place on the Ward Returns, marking another day in the ebb and flow of hospital life. Ethel remained a silent witness to the passage of time, her presence a poignant reminder of the fragility and resilience that define the human experience.

Bay Ward
Bay Ward: 27 beds.
Beds Occupied: 26. Beds Empty: 1.
Admissions: 0. Discharges: 0. On leave: 0. Deceased: 1.

My Diary

I've known St Luke's forever. I've grown up hearing stories about the hospital. It's always been a big part of my life, I've attended fêtes, coffee mornings, bonfire nights, and Christmas carol services for as long as I can remember.

I've never really thought about where I wanted to work. I just knew I'd end up working there. There was no other option for me, really. I loved being a nursing assistant, and doing my training is a natural step forward. I love being part of the hospital community. It's a real home from home for me.

With Mum a domestic supervisor, my two aunties registered nurses, my cousin a chef, and my Uncle Tim a maintenance man. Our family could have shares in the place!

It'll be a sad day when the hospital closes. The move to care in the community is coming. I wonder what will happen to the patients and the staff? I wonder what will happen to St Luke's? Rumour has it that it will be converted into luxury flats and apartments.

S Group reunion night out tomorrow—I can't wait to see everyone. It's been a while since our last bash. I won't drink so much this time. I'm getting too old for hangovers and shenanigans. Besides, Tom and Lizzie are staying at Joe's this weekend, so I've arranged to work some extra bank shifts. I'm looking forward to working with Maureen and Dave again on Myrtle Ward.

3
BANK NURSING

"When you're a nurse, you know that every day you will touch a life, or a life will touch yours."
Unknown

St Luke's used a 'bank' of nurses employed directly by the hospital on a flexible basis instead of agency nurses. We were part of an internal pool that the hospital could draw from to fill temporary staffing shortages, cover absences, or handle fluctuations in patient numbers. Unlike agency nurses, who were contracted through expensive external agencies, bank nurses had a direct employment relationship with the hospital, offering more stability and integration with the hospital's policies and procedures.

The predictability of a nine-to-five office job held little appeal for me. The thought of being confined to the monotonous routine of cubicles and fluorescent lighting seemed stifling compared to the dynamic environment of the hospital, where each shift brought new challenges and opportunities to make a difference.

The early morning shifts signaled the start of a bustling day, where the hospital corridors buzzed with activity long before the city stirred awake. I've always been an early riser, so starting at 7 am and working until 2:30 pm suited me. I like to think I navigated the frenetic pace with humour and good heart.

The late shifts had a different pace and offered us a chance to embrace the quietude of twilight, tending to the needs of patients as the day waned into evening. Maintaining a steadfast presence, working from 1:30 pm and finishing at 8 pm, there was an ebb and flow of emergencies, admissions, and discharges.

The night shifts were a realm unto themselves. While the outside world slumbered, we kept vigil through the wee hours. It was a long night, from 7:30 pm until 7:30 am, navigating the shadows and darkness with quiet determination, despite our fatigue and exhaustion.

Each shift held its own appeal, and I usually found some kind of purpose and meaning in my days. The knowledge that I was at least trying to make a difference motivated me.

My employment status as part of the bank staff afforded me flexibility within the hospital's workforce. While some of my colleagues adhered to regular shift patterns, my inability to commit to such rigidity due to my personal circumstances made me an invaluable asset to the institution. I think I learned to be adaptable and was able to transition between departments and wards as the needs of the hospital dictated. When wards found themselves short-staffed due to unforeseen circumstances or seasonal fluctuations, we stepped in, ensuring continuity of care, and upholding the hospital's commitment to excellence.

Holidays and weekends were no exception—if the children were staying at Joe's, I was generally able to stand in wherever I was needed at short notice. I accepted the variety and unpredictability of shift work with open arms.

Working for the bank gave me the luxury and freedom to choose my shifts according to my preferences, the trade-off came in the form of forfeiting paid holiday and sick time benefits.

The challenging, fast-paced, and deeply rewarding nature of mental health nursing resonated with me. The dynamic environment of mental health care ensured that there was always something new unfolding—whether it was encountering new patients with unique backgrounds and experiences, welcoming fresh faces among the staff, or delving into the intricacies of new and evolving therapeutic approaches and treatments. The variety in my role, especially working across so many wards and departments, kept me engaged and motivated. I never got complacent because I was always somewhere different.

As a single mum, I appreciated the opportunity to work, and I was content with the arrangement for the time being. I had positive relationships with colleagues across various wards and departments, and I thrived in the hospital environment.

Every day brought opportunities to learn and grow, and although I was often frustrated with management, staff shortages, and the internal and personal politics at the hospital, I never experienced a dull moment. I was never bored.

4
DAPHNE

"Our envy always lasts longer than the happiness of those we envy."
Heraclitus

I started work as a nursing assistant and then, encouraged by Barbara, I decided to apply for nurse training. Not everyone in the hospital was supportive of my plans.

Daphne, an experienced nursing assistant with a penchant for believing she knew everything there was to know about nursing, was particularly vocal and critical of me. "Why don't you just stay as you are? Stay a nursing assistant," she sneered. Her negativity was palpable. "Bloody trained staff! You'll be getting ideas above your station. Who do you think you are?"

Her disposition was consistently negative and opinionated. She viewed the latest ideas with disdain, often rolling her eyes and dismissing them with a curt statement: "We did that before! It didn't work then, and it ain't gonna work now!"

Her resistance to change and her belief in the superiority of her own knowledge created a challenging environment for those, like me, who sought to introduce innovation and progress. She was a challenge to work with, and her negativity could influence the whole team.

Mum told me to ignore her. "You know what she's like. She's jealous of you, Claire. She fancies herself as a Matron, Daphne does. Stand up for yourself."

I tried to avoid Daphne when I could. I felt threatened and undermined by her.

One Sunday, we had to take a break together. The canteen was closed, so we retreated to the small staff room on the ward. As soon as we settled in and the door was closed, she wasted no time in fixing a critical eye on me.

"When do you start your training then?" she grumbled, lighting a cigarette and squinting through the smoke haze at me.

Cringing, I replied, "In March," and kept my gaze fixed on a *Woman's Weekly* magazine, avoiding direct eye contact and wishing myself out of there.

"Ooooh. March, is it? Get you! Don't think you can come back here bossing me about when you're one of the Trained," she said, punctuating each word with a jab of her lit cigarette.

I shrugged and replied, "I like to think I'll be a good nurse, Daph. The last thing on my mind would be to boss you about. As if."

Daphne leaned in towards me, her face bitter. "I'll tell you what, Claire. In my opinion, a sign of a good nurse is one that can hold a fag and a sandwich with one hand and wipe someone's arse at the same time. When you can do that, without throwing up, you let me know. Then, and only then, will you be a good nurse."

"Wow. I always wondered what your yardstick was," I quipped, trying to diffuse the tension that hung in the air. I couldn't resist a touch of sarcasm, adding, "I'll remember that Daph. And... exactly what sort of sandwich is it that I'd have to eat to be a good nurse in your book?"

Daphne, momentarily caught off guard, recovered with a sly grin, replying menacingly, "Shit. Shit with sugar on!"

Our eyes locked, but now red-faced and trying not to laugh, I managed to say, "Seriously, is that your favourite sandwich, Daph? Shit? Shit with sugar on?"

Realising the absurdity of her statement, she sniggered, the smoke from her cigarette causing her to cough and gasp for breath. "You bet it is," she sniggered. "But don't spread it around."

We both grinned. The tension eased, replaced by a shared amusement and newfound respect for each other.

My Diary

Bloody Daphne! Always wanting to have a go! She's a right know-all-knows-nothing. I'll give her a shit sandwich one of these days! Part of me feels sorry for her. Always having to have a go at someone. Mum said she's had a hard life, and that's what makes her such a miserable and opinionated old goat. She does make me laugh, though. She's a character. One of 'The Trained'! I've got a long way to go until then. A sandwich and a fag in one hand and wipe someone's arse with the other hand! Blimey. What a picture.

5
THE MAIN ENTRANCE

"How many desolate creatures on the earth have learnt the simple dues of fellowship and social comfort, in a hospital?"
Elizabeth Barrett Browning, Lady Geraldine's Courtship

The main entrance to the hospital always buzzed with activity, a constant hive of movement and energy. As you passed under the huge arch and through the imposing double doors, visitors were greeted by a spacious red, white, and black tiled reception area.

The whole reception hub served as a fascinating window into the workings and personalities of St Luke's.

To the immediate left of the entrance, the porter's lodge commanded a central vantage point for enquiries, assistance, and vigilant monitoring of the hospital's movements and deliveries. The watchful eyes of the portering team captured and recorded every detail of life in the hospital.

Corridors branched off from the square, with clear signage pointing the way to the different wings, wards, and departments.

In the far-left corner, opposite the porter's lodge, was the hospital shop—a cherished establishment run by the dedicated ladies of the Friends of St Luke's.

Open daily from 9am to 1pm, their services were a vital lifeline for the whole hospital community. Inside, the shelves brimmed with essential items and indulgent treats. Daily newspapers and magazines provided a link to the outside world for patients and visitors. Toiletries ensured comfort and convenience for patients during their stay. Chocolates, sweets, and crisps tempted every passerby. Coffee, tea, and soft drinks were served, each accompanied by a complimentary packet of two biscuits.

On the right side of the reception area, a row of mismatched, tired chairs formed a makeshift waiting area. The floor tiles were worn in places, tea-stained, and marked with burnt patches where cigarettes had been dropped or stubbed out.

Aluminium ashtrays, overflowing with cigarette butts, and half-drunk cups of cold tea sat discarded under the chairs. Visitors, staff, and patients alike sat patiently in the smoky area, waiting their turn for appointments or passing the time, having a drink, a smoke, and a chat before catching the bus into the city.

The bus stop, conveniently located just outside the main entrance, provided easy access for those travelling to and from the hospital.

For many, the main entrance was not just a reception area, but a place to connect with each other and to watch the comings and goings of staff, visitors, and patients. Even the most mundane moments were interesting.

A core group of patients had made it their unofficial gathering place. Whether they were seated on the chairs inside, engaged in conversation, or meandering about outside, they seemed to be a constant presence, and their familiar faces lent a sense of continuity to the ever-changing hospital environment.

Between them, they possessed an uncanny ability to recall the names of all the staff and fellow patients, and they greeted everyone warmly. If they happened upon someone whose name escaped them, they would extend a courteous, "Good morning, Sir," or "Afternoon, Missus," ensuring that everyone felt acknowledged and welcomed in their shared space.

Some patients appeared withdrawn, their gaze distant and their movements hesitant. Clad in plain, often worn-out clothing, they exuded an air of quiet resignation, perhaps weighed down by the burden of their mental health struggles and institutionalisation.

Others displayed a restless energy, their movements erratic and their expressions animated. These individuals seemed to teeter on the edge of agitation, their minds racing with thoughts and emotions beyond their control. Their clothing was often dishevelled, reflecting their inner turmoil.

Among the characters was Old Tom, always dressed in a grey suit, shirt, and spotted tie. Sat next to him was his friend Tilly, a small, round lady, dressed in floral attire, wearing liberally applied shocking pink lipstick and bright blue eyeshadow. Both in their seventies, they spent their time holding hands and drinking tea together.

Tom and Tilly both exhibited side effects of long-term use of medication. Tardive dyskinesia, a neurological disorder characterised by involuntary movements, was commonly associated with the long-term use of certain antipsychotic medications. As they sat chatting, their repetitive, involuntary movements, grimacing, tongue protrusion, lip-smacking, and rapid blinking were obvious.

Tilly gazed affectionately at Tom. She was fiercely protective of their relationship and would assert her claim with a playful yell of "Get away from my boyfriend!" whenever anyone dared to get too close to him.

Tom, amused by her antics, would respond with pride, puffing out his chest, reassuring her, "You're the only one for me, my Tilly."

In response, Tilly would dissolve into hysterical giggles like a lovestruck teenager.

Clive had epilepsy and wore a leather helmet as a form of protection against head injuries. The helmet was designed to provide cushioning and support to minimise the risk of significant injury if he were to fall during a seizure.

Clive's frequent seizures were a source of concern for both him and his caregivers. Standing at an imposing height of six feet six inches, he had experienced several severe injuries in the past. The leather helmet offered him a renewed sense of security.

With his helmet snugly in place, Clive felt able to participate in his daily activities with greater assurance, knowing that he had an additional safeguard against potential head injuries. The helmet enabled him to navigate his daily life with increased confidence and peace of mind.

The use of leather helmets for epilepsy patients has become less common over time, but they were once a common sight in hospitals and care facilities.

Clive had developed a keen awareness of his body's signals. He could often sense when a seizure was imminent, and when he felt the telltale signs, he would take action to protect himself. With remarkable self-awareness, he would lie down and announce loudly, "I'm having a fit."

This proactive approach not only helped ensure his safety but also enabled those around him to quickly summon support. If a seizure occurred in the main entrance, fellow patients like Tom, Tilly, and others would immediately raise their voices, calling out to the porters in the nearby lodge.

"Clive's having a fit! Oi! Oi! Someone call the Ward!"

In a solitary chair nestled in the corner of the reception area sat Peter, like a monumental Buddha, his chubby presence commanding attention despite his peaceful slumber.

Peter's huge belly caused the buttons on his grubby shirt to strain. His baggy black trousers were held up with red braces. His face was battered like a boxer who'd fought countless opponents in the ring. His features told a story of the battles he'd fought and the blows he'd endured. His nose had been broken umpteen times, his ears like cauliflowers, hardened and swollen from years of grappling and combat.

As Peter's deep snores reverberated through the room, people looked and smiled and shook their heads as they passed him. Despite his sleepy and serene appearance, he had an extensive and troubled forensic history of violence and robbery.

His schizophrenia and years of high-dose, high-potency medications—while quelling the once-chaotic storm of delusions and hallucinations—had left him in a deficit state, with a disappearance of positive symptoms, such as delusions and hallucinations, and an increase in negative symptoms, such as social withdrawal, affective flattening, and lack of motivation. His diagnosis at this time was written in red capital letters across the top of his case notes: "burnt-out schizophrenic."

Isolated by the weight of his past and the stigma surrounding his condition, Peter had lost contact with family members and had no visitors. His reputation and occasional outbursts of disagreement had effectively erected barriers around him, keeping potential friendships at bay. The fear of inadvertently triggering a volatile response kept many at arm's length, and they left Peter to navigate his existence alone.

Despite the barriers that kept others away, he found a ray of companionship in Keith, the head porter. Keith saw beyond the walls of stigma and fear, and sometimes during his break would join Peter to share a cup of tea, a biscuit, and some light-hearted banter.

Their conversations, though repetitive at times, were a source of comfort and fun for both men. They covered topics ranging from football to gardening, and even the latest news headlines. Despite his solitary demeanour, Peter revealed a surprising depth of knowledge and insight that Keith admired and encouraged.

Peter and Keith shared some longstanding jokes between them.

Without fail, every day Keith would ask, "How are you doing, Peter, me old cock sparrow?"

To which Peter would reply with a wry grin, "Fine thanks, but I'd rather have a bottle in front of me than a frontal lobotomy."

Both men would chuckle.

Peter would pipe up each day, "Here, Keith. I know what words you should have on your gravestone."

"What's that then, Peter?" Keith would respond with a blank face.

"Underneath this sod lies another."

Despite the repetition, both men would burst out laughing as if hearing the jokes for the very first time, relishing in their own private craic. Peter would amuse himself by muttering inaudibly under his breath. When an unsuspecting person apologised for not hearing him and asked him to repeat himself, he would glare at them in mock anger and shout, "I've never had paranoid delusions. Somebody told me I did, but I know they're lying." His face would then crease with laughter at his own joke, turning red as his chuckles turned to coughing.

From the lodge, Keith maintained a friendly and watchful eye over Peter, attuned to the subtle shifts in his mood.

When the decision was made for Peter to transition to the community, resistance flared within him, manifesting in waves of anger and frustration. The prospect of leaving behind the familiar surroundings of the hospital filled him with panic.

In the face of Peter's vehement protests, Keith was able to step forward to extend a listening ear and compassionate support. Through their heartfelt conversations about his fears for the future, Peter gradually softened, his resistance yielding to acceptance. The staff breathed a collective sigh of relief, grateful for Keith's intervention and the invaluable role he played in easing Peter's transition.

Aleksy and Tomasz were Polish citizens who had served in the Polish Armed Forces during the war and subsequently settled in the UK after World War II. Both had experienced trauma and mental health issues because of their wartime experiences. The challenges in repatriating displaced persons to their home countries due to a range of factors, such as political instability, family separation, and personal circumstances, meant that Aleksy and Tomasz were unable to return to Poland and so remained at St Luke's.

They faced significant language and cultural barriers within the healthcare system and struggled to communicate directly with staff members due to language differences and a lack of trust. As a result, they isolated themselves and primarily interacted with each other, forming their own tight-knit community of two within the hospital.

Both men were small in stature, thin and weather-beaten, and their days were spent scouring the floors and grounds of the hospital in search of discarded cigarette butts. Their scavenging allowed them to collect enough tobacco to roll their own cigarettes using cigarette papers, finding friendship in the act of smoking and sharing cigarettes with one another.

Soon after their relocation to a community home, Aleksy died. Several weeks later, Tomasz, unable to endure the loss of his companion, also passed away. It was speculated by some that Tomasz's death was a result of profound loneliness.

Josie stood out among the regular patients in the reception area as the loudest and most flamboyant. With her wild auburn curly hair, vibrant personality, and mismatched clothing, she strode around the hospital with a wide-legged gait, swaying from side to side and repeating, "Bah bah bah. Are the nurses alright? Bah bah bah. Are the nurses alright?" rhythmically as she moved.

Her learning disability was obvious, as was her lack of teeth. A stark reminder of the outdated practice of 'teeth clearance' that she'd undergone in the 1970s. This controversial procedure, intended to prevent patients biting themselves and others, had left Josie with long-term physical and psychological consequences, robbing her of her natural teeth. The practice rightly raised ethical concerns about patient rights and medical interventions.

Like a clumsy butterfly, Josie flitted noisily in and out of wards and departments, the library, the church, the kitchens, the laundry—wherever she found an unlocked door. She was well known for her unpredictable antics.

Sometimes she was offered a cup of tea, which she slurped greedily, her enthusiasm for the beverage often resulting in more spillage than sipping, much to the annoyance of those around her.

Her presence in the hospital was not always welcome. Many staff members found her loud and intrusive behaviour intolerable, prompting them to swiftly usher her out the door whenever she overstayed her welcome.

Josie seemed to thrive on confrontation, often causing a scene if she was escorted away, deliberately slamming doors and toppling furniture in her wake.

When she was unceremoniously ejected from the department, she would emit a high-pitched scream, and a maniacal yell, then run off laughing and cackling down the corridor. "Are the nurses alright?"

Beneath her exuberant exterior lay a tumultuous world of inner struggles and unspoken pain. She never stayed anywhere for long, wandering endlessly, always returning to her own ward for meals and bedtime, then back to the main entrance. One thing was for certain: Josie's adventures in the hospital were always guaranteed to keep everyone on their toes.

Josie found solace in smoking. Often seen with lit cigarettes in both hands and another tucked behind her ear, smoking was a habit she clung to fervently.

Her desperate need for cigarettes led her to engage in risky and inappropriate behaviours, putting herself in vulnerable situations. When her supply ran low, she resorted to extreme measures, including begging, borrowing, or even stealing cigarettes from fellow patients or staff. Her lack of inhibition and understanding of social boundaries was evident in her brazen attempts to procure cigarettes.

At the bus queue, she would loudly proposition others, offering sexual favours in exchange for a smoke. "Give us a fag, I'll give you a shag," she would shout at the bus queue. "Go on. I'll give you a hand job. You want me to lick it, do you? Look, I've got no teeth! I'll bite it and suck it all you want. Are the nurses alright?"

Her crude and explicit offers shocked those around her, highlighting her complete lack of self-awareness and disregard for social boundaries or personal safety.

Josie's dependence on cigarettes left her susceptible to exploitation, and her naivety and lack of awareness of the dangers posed by her actions made her an easy target for manipulation by others. She sustained frequent injuries, often visible as black eyes or grazed knees, which raised eyebrows among the hospital staff. Despite their probing questions, she remained tight-lipped about how she obtained them. Attempts to shield her from harm by confining her to the ward only exacerbated her distress.

Josie had boundless energy, and the confines of the ward suffocated her restless spirit. She became like a caged animal, exhibiting extreme behaviours: pacing, hitting herself, pulling her hair, lashing out at staff, shouting obscenities, and smearing the walls of her room with faeces. Each action was a manifestation of her profound turmoil and her desperate need for freedom, understanding, and support.

While letting her roam freely was far from ideal, it was preferable to the torment of confinement. Staff tried and failed to educate her about staying safe. Thankfully, Josie did take one key piece of advice onboard and remained within the hospital grounds. She never attempted to leave or board the bus.

Amidst the chaos of Josie's disruptive escapades, her poignant and recurring enquiry resonated: "Are the nurses alright?" I always thought that her question reflected a genuine concern for the well-being of those who selflessly devote themselves to caring for others, transcending mere curiosity.

The truth is that despite everything, we nurses remain unwavering in our commitment, tirelessly attending to our patients with steadfast dedication. Our resilience is evident as we work, often without complaint, our uniforms blending us into a collective entity, each of us seemingly reduced to a mere number in the system. Nurses are the unsung heroes, the backbone of the hospital.

Beneath the uniformity lies a profound humanity. Each nurse carries their own burdens, facing life's challenges and uncertainties. Do we receive the recognition and support we deserve for our tireless efforts? Is our dedication truly valued?

Josie's question lingers, echoing through the hospital corridors. I find myself agreeing with her. Does anyone genuinely stop to wonder, ***Are the nurses alright?***

6
MATRON BAIN

> "The goal is not to be liked, it's to be respected."
> Unknown

It was Saturday afternoon, and I parked my old dark blue Ford Fiesta in the closest spot to the main entrance, ensuring it was securely locked before walking purposefully across the expanse of the car park, heading towards the imposing, black-painted front doors of the hospital.

Up the steps, under the arch and through the doors, I smiled at the familiar patients in the main entrance and acknowledged the porters with a wave as I headed towards the back-office (*3). No one knew why it was called the 'back-office'. Given its position at the front of the hospital in this mental institution, it seemed entirely appropriate to be so strangely named, and it always made me smile.

New nurses and students would often ask, "Why is it called the back-office when it is at the front?" Older nurses would smile and shake their heads, shrug, and say, "It just is." "Arse about face, like everything else in this place!"

As you walked from the car park across the tarmac drive, towards the entrance, you could just see the top of the Nursing Officer or Matron's head in the back-office window if they were sitting at the desk.

Occasionally, they'd stand watching from the window as staff reported for duty. While this could make you feel uncomfortable, it also meant that you could prepare yourself in advance for the reception you were likely to receive.

Matron Bain commanded the day's duties with her imposing presence. She was a formidable figure with a no-nonsense demeanour and a distinctly clipped, straight-to-the-point manner of speaking that could be intimidating. Highly seasoned and sharp-witted, Matron left no room for ambiguity or error in her administration of the hospital.

Fortunately for me, Matron Bain seemed to like me. As I tapped lightly on the door to inquire about my shift assignment for the day, she looked up from the 'Midnight

Returns' (*4) document spread across her desk. With a practiced motion, she removed her glasses, placing them neatly aside before offering a warm smile.

"Ah, Claire, how're you doing?" said Matron Bain with a smile. "How are your wee ones? All okay, I hope?"

"All good, thank you, Matron. Growing like weeds, the pair of them."

That brief exchange, amidst the controlled chaos of the hospital's daily operations, highlighted our sense of mutual respect. It confirmed the delicate balance of authority and understanding that defined our professional relationship.

Matron Bain smiled, nodded, then swiftly transitioned from pleasantries to a more pragmatic demeanour. "Right, Nurse Taylor," she began briskly, assuming a tone of authority, "you're assigned to Bluebell this afternoon. We have twenty-four patients in, and as far as I'm aware, all is quiet. You'll be taking over from Staff Nurse Lucy Wilson, and you'll be in charge for the duration of your shift. Unfortunately, Senior Staff Nurse Kitts has called in sick... yet again. Apologies for the inconvenience. I'm on a long day, so I'll check in with you later. If you encounter any issues, don't hesitate to bleep me."

With that, Matron conveyed both the urgency and responsibility inherent in the hospital, setting her clear expectations for me as I assumed my duties on Bluebell Ward.

She then turned her attention back to the Returns sheets in front of her, and I realised I'd been dismissed. I said, "Thank you, Matron," then set off along the corridor to Bluebell Ward, nodding to other bank staff coming in for the late shift and reporting for duty to the back-office.

The ritual of completing the Ward Return at the end of every late shift and night shift punctuated the rhythm of hospital life, signaling the completion of another shift of patient care. The completed Ward Return was then entrusted to a willing nursing assistant, a courier tasked with delivering the document to the back-office in a timely manner.

Amidst the flurry of activity that accompanied the transition between shifts, the urgency of the task was palpable, stressed by the charge nurse's emphatic instruction: "Quick! Quick! Take this upstairs to the back-office, quick as you can!" The nursing assistant sprang into action, navigating the labyrinthine corridors of the hospital with determination. Reaching the back-office, they delivered the Ward Return into the waiting hands of the Nursing Officer or into the office letterbox.

      The task offered them a welcome reprieve from the intensity of their duties and a chance to connect with colleagues from other wards and departments. Sometimes, they took a cheeky cigarette break on the way back, stealing away to the hospital's designated smoking area for a few precious moments of respite. With each hurried puff, they momentarily disconnected from the demands of their role in the ritual of nicotine and contemplation.

7
LEN

> *"Flush all your worries away."*
> *Unknown*

Bluebell Ward. Late Shift.
Psychogeriatric Ward. Mixed sex. 34 beds.

The traditional layout of Bluebell Ward was common to wards of this era, and I liked working there. The main door to the ward remained securely locked, for safety and security. We all had a universal hospital key that held the means to access most doors within the ward, giving us seamless movement and a swift response to patient needs if required.

For visitors seeking entry, there was a simple ritual. When they rang the doorbell, their presence was announced, and they stood, their silhouette framed by the reinforced glass door as they awaited admission. A passing member of the hospital staff, perhaps a nurse, doctor, or domestic, would then pause in their duties to extend a welcome, unlocking the door and ushering the visitor into the sanctuary of Bluebell Ward. In this dance of accessibility and vigilance, the ward stood as a bastion of care, its doors opening to visitors while also safeguarding the privacy of its inhabitants.

The main living room of Bluebell Ward unfolded as a vibrant tableau of functionality. Its expansive red and cream checkered lino floor served as a durable foundation, grounding the space with an attempt at warmth.

High-backed, blue and green fully washable vinyl armchairs, designed for ease of maintenance, formed clusters around a television, commanding attention with its ceaseless stream of programmes.

At the opposite end, round dining tables adorned in gingham green and white plastic tablecloths beckoned residents to communal meals and social gatherings. Each table boasted an orange plastic vase, filled with multi-coloured plastic flowers stiffly arranged at the centre showing an attempt at homeyness amidst the utilitarian surroundings.

At the heart of the room, the office stood as a central hub, its half-glazed facade offering a panoramic vista of the whole ward's activities. Affectionately dubbed 'the fishbowl', the office provided a vantage point where we could see the comings and goings of residents.

From this pivotal point, doors branched out to various essential spaces—the dormitory, clinic room, interview room, toilet block, sluice, and staff room.

Within the intimate confines of the office, our clinical insights were shared, strategies devised, and the day-to-day workings of Bluebell Ward rhythmically managed with informal discussions, meetings, and handovers (*5).

Staff Nurse Lucy Wilson delivered today's handover to me and the rest of the afternoon shift with remarkable efficiency. She opted for clear communication without relying heavily on abbreviations, providing updates on the twenty-four patients under their care. The majority being described simply as 'no change,' indicating stability in their conditions. The exception was Len, who stood out as he was noted to be 'on the wander' for the day.

As we nodded in acknowledgment during the handover, our attention was drawn to Len, who appeared right on cue, meandering past us.

Our collective understanding of Len's condition was evident, and we smiled and nodded at each other in acknowledgment.

Len mooched quietly around the ward; his gentle demeanour seemed to belie the weight of his circumstances. The loss of his wife, coupled with his own declining health, had created a palpable sense of solitude around him. His life as an accountant in the city now felt like a distant memory, replaced by the quiet hum of Bluebell Ward. Len picked up objects, rearranging them, and muttered softly to himself as he wandered. His bright blue eyes still held a glimmer of the vitality that once defined him but were clouded with sadness.

When his wife died, and with no one around to look after him, Len's health and mind had deteriorated rapidly. Without children or family nearby, his journey through Parkinson's disease felt like a solitary voyage. It's such a cruel progressive brain disorder, causing unintended or uncontrollable movements, like shaking, stiffness, and difficulty with balance and coordination.

As Len's disease progressed, he had difficulty walking and talking, gradually worsening over time. He wore a white shirt, grey trousers, a beige cardigan, and slippers. His navy slippers were stained with dried-on, old, forgotten blobs of food. He shuffled along, almost tripping occasionally, and leaning slightly to one side.

As the morning shift ended, staff were eager to transition out of their professional roles and into the comfort of their civilian clothes. With the handover process concluded, they retreated to the staff room, where they could shed their uniforms and unwind after a demanding shift (*6).

As the team changed out of their uniforms and prepared to leave, the staff room buzzed with the hum of camaraderie. As soon as they had exchanged their polyester dresses and sensible black shoes for their comfortable civilian clothes, trainers, and boots, they left in a flurry of chatter and cheery waves and calls of:

"Have a good shift!"

"See you tomorrow!"

"I'm on a week's leave now, woohoo!"

After the handover, I discussed the diary entries with the team and assigned tasks and duties to each person.

The afternoon shift unfolded as usual with supervised baths for some of the patients. Hair was washed, nails trimmed, bodies soaped and bathed, dried, and powdered. Patients were then made ready for bed in clean nightwear, dressing gowns, and slippers to save them getting dressed then undressed again at bedtime.

The visiting hours from 3 to 5 pm brought a sense of familiarity and routine to the ward, as a dedicated group of regular visitors arrived to spend time with their loved ones. With bouquets of flowers for the patients and chocolates for the staff, they brought warmth and comfort to the clinical environment, infusing the ward with a touch of home and news from outside. As they settled into their customary seats, the regular visitors assumed their roles as vigilant observers, with watchful eyes tracking the movements and interactions of both patients and staff alike. With a keen sense of awareness, they absorbed the nuances of the ward's atmosphere, attuned to the needs and well-being of their beloved family members.

Occasionally, snippets of conversation would float through the air as the visitors' exchanged comments amongst themselves or engaged in polite banter with the nurses. Their presence served as a gentle reminder of the interconnectedness of the hospital community, bridging the gap between patient and caregiver with empathy and understanding. With their unwavering support and steadfast presence, the regular visitors became integral members of our hospital family.

The patients drifted in and out of wakefulness or stared into the distance, lost in their thoughts in the presence of their loved ones.

The pattern of visits described reflects the poignant journey experienced by both patients and their loved ones as they navigated the complexities of illness and decline. Initially, the frequency of visits was marked by a sense of urgency and concern, with family members and friends rallying around the patient during their time of need. As the patient's health deteriorated and their ability to interact diminished, visits tended to become less frequent, mirroring the shifting dynamics of the patient's condition and the evolving emotional landscape of their loved ones.

Some visitors continued to maintain a regular presence, a testimony to the enduring bond shared with the patient despite the challenges they faced. Others visited on special occasions such as birthdays or holidays only.

Throughout this emotional journey, the ward staff played a vital role in providing support and comfort to both patients and their visitors. We helped them come to terms with the inevitable decline and demise of their loved ones, offering a listening ear and a shoulder to lean on during moments of grief and sorrow.

It was painful to see devoted partners visiting their lifelong companions, only to be met with confusion or detachment. The heartbreaking toll of illness and decline was underscored by questions like, "Who are you? Where is my husband?"

Many of the patients had no visitors at all.

At 3 o'clock, a comforting daily ritual unfolded. Afternoon tea and biscuits were served, first for the patients and then for the staff, a welcome reprieve from the rigours of the day.

Trays laden with tea and an assortment of biscuits made their rounds, offering an indulgent break amidst the clinical setting. Patients savoured the simple pleasure of tea and biscuits, their spirits uplifted by the familiar flavours and gestures of kindness from the nursing staff.

Once the patients had been attended to, we took our tea break. In pairs, we retreated from the bustling ward, seeking refuge in the cosy confines of the staff room. Here, amidst the aroma of brewing tea and the inviting spread of malted milk, chocolate digestives, and Rich Tea biscuits, we took a break from the demands of our duties.

Conversations flowed freely as we shared stories, exchanged laughter, and forged bonds of friendship over steaming cups of tea and the comforting crunch of biscuits. In these moments of connection, the stresses of the day were put aside, replaced by a sense of solidarity and shared purpose that fortified our resolve for the tasks that lay ahead.

Tasks like the 'toilet round,' which occurred before and after each meal, mid-morning, mid-afternoon, and before bedtime (*7).

I fondly recall attending a lively lecture delivered by Dr Rahman, an eminent physician and a captivating storyteller who seamlessly interwove graphic pictures and anecdotes into his lectures. Amidst his engaging narrative, one crucial message resonated profoundly: the paramount importance of diligently recording and monitoring the bowel habits of patients, particularly when they lacked the capacity to do so themselves.

In the lecture hall, the physician's words echoed with resonance, underscoring the significance of this seemingly mundane aspect of patient care. With clarity and conviction, he illuminated the profound implications that subtle changes in bowel habits could hold for a patient's health and well-being, serving as a window into underlying conditions and potential complications.

For me, the lecture served as more than a mere academic exercise. It was a poignant reminder of the need for holistic patient care and a warning not to forget the basics. An awareness and vigilance around bowel habits is important, to proactively identify issues, intervene promptly, and optimise the quality of care provided to vulnerable patients.

Dr Rahman was a small man. A diminutive figure with round spectacles perched on his nose, framing eyes that sparkled with intellectual curiosity. His most distinctive feature, however, was his grey handlebar moustache that lent him an air of eccentricity.

During his lectures, he would pause, twirling his moustache with deliberate finesse. With a thoughtful gaze fixed ahead, he seemed to ponder the weight of his words, each twirl punctuating the silence before he resumed his discourse with renewed vigour.

For S Group, this idiosyncratic gesture was a quirk that endeared him to us. Beyond the confines of academia, his presence illuminated the lecture hall, infusing each session with a blend of humour and charm that left an indelible impression on all who had the privilege to listen.

It was figures like him—quirky, passionate, and deeply committed to their craft—who breathed life into our pursuit of knowledge, inspiring us to embrace curiosity and interest in our careers. As his memorable lecture neared its conclusion, Dr Rahman posed a thought-provoking question to the group: "Which organ is the Boss?" His inquiry hung in the air, sparking anticipation and curiosity among us. We looked at each other, raising our eyebrows and smiling.

In a surprising twist, he embarked on a theatrical journey, adopting a range of voices to personify each organ in the body. With animated gestures and infectious energy, he breathed life into the organs, transforming the lecture hall into a vibrant stage where the inner workings of the human body came alive.

From the authoritative voice of the brain, commanding and decisive, to the rhythmic cadence of the heart, pulsating with life and vitality, Dr Rahman wove a captivating narrative that captured his audience's imagination.

Each organ emerged as a distinct character, its role and significance within the intricate web of human physiology illuminated with clarity and humour.

All the organs of the body were having a meeting, trying to decide who was the one in charge...

"I should be in charge," said the brain, "because I run all the body's systems, so without me, nothing would happen."

"I should be in charge," said the blood, "because I circulate oxygen all over, so without me, you'd waste away."

"I should be in charge," said the stomach, "because I process food and give you all energy."

"I should be in charge," said the legs, "because I carry the body wherever it needs to go."

"I should be in charge," said the eyes, "because I allow the body to see where it goes."

"I should be in charge," said the rectum, "because I am responsible for waste removal."

All the other body parts laughed at the rectum and insulted him, so in a huff, he shut down tight.

Within a few days, the brain had a terrible headache, the stomach was bloated, the legs got wobbly, the eyes got watery, and the blood became toxic. Soon they all agreed that the rectum should indeed be The Boss.

Dr Rahman concluded his narrative with a flourish, ensuring that the message resonated with his audience before punctuating the tale with a wry joke: "And the moral of this story, ladies and gentlemen?" he quipped, a mischievous glint dancing in his eyes. "Even though the others do all the work... the Asshole is usually in charge. Remember that! *The Asshole.*"

His unexpected punchline elicited a ripple of laughter and amusement throughout the room. In his light-hearted jest, the physician skillfully conveyed a profound truth, using humour as a vehicle to highlight the intricate dynamics of the human body to us in a manner that was both memorable and relatable.

In this moment of playful exploration, Dr Rahman transcended the confines of traditional lecture dynamics, inviting us, his audience, to engage with the subject matter on a deeper, more personal level.

His innovative approach sparked conversations, ignited our curiosity, and left an indelible mark on all of us who had the privilege to witness his unique style of teaching. Amidst the laughter, however, lingered a deeper appreciation for the complexities of human physiology and the remarkable synergy that defines the interplay of its various components.

Through his deft storytelling and comedic timing, he left us not only entertained but also enlightened, instilling an impression that transcended the confines of the lecture hall. He left the lecture theatre with a flourish, grinning and twizzling his moustache gleefully.

It was a truly memorable lecture.

After the toilet round, we helped all patients to sit up at the dining tables in preparation for supper at 5 pm. For those who were chronically disabled and unable to sit on a standard dining chair, specially designed reclining mobile chairs known as 'Buxtons' were used. These were dark red or dark green vinyl-covered chairs. They had a tubular metal frame, four braked castors, calf supports, a fold-up footboard, and angle-lipped tray table.

They also had a reclining mechanism that posed a potential hazard if not handled with care. If staff failed to provide them with adequate warning before tipping the chairs back for manoeuvring, the poor patients could unexpectedly find themselves propelled backwards, their perspective shifting abruptly as they suddenly gazed up at the celling.

The meals at St Luke's were standard hospital fare (*8) with a two-week rotating menu that emerged from the bustling kitchens, orchestrated by a dedicated band of chefs, many of whom had honed their craft within the institution since leaving school. Their collective expertise and familiarity with the hospital's culinary landscape formed the cornerstone of meal preparation and service.

The 'hot trolley' made its grand daily entrance onto each ward, heralding the imminent arrival of lunchtime and suppertime. This formidable contraption, a large and sturdy steel box on wheels, held within its depths the promise of nourishing meals.

The hot trolley was wheeled into place, plugged in, and started heating the meals inside. Each shelf brimmed with neatly arranged cardboard trays. Each individual tray was labelled with its contents. In the hour or so that followed, the trolley hummed softly, its internal heating system working to ensure that each tray of food reached the optimal temperature for serving. The aroma permeated the ward slowly, eliciting anticipation from the patients.

The moment of truth arrived as the kitchen porter or chef made their appearance on the ward. Armed with a kitchen thermometer, they embarked on a meticulous inspection, probing each cardboard tray with precision to ascertain whether its contents had been adequately heated through. With a practiced eye and a nod of approval, they gave the nearest nurse the thumbs-up sign—a universal gesture of readiness and assurance.

With their mission accomplished, the kitchen porter or chef retreated through the main door, heading swiftly to another ward. In their wake, the hot trolley stood as a beacon of culinary delight, its contents primed and ready to offer nourishment to all who gathered around its steaming trays.

The television was always turned off while the patients were eating meals. As usual, when supper was finished, they were guided or helped back to sit in the more comfortable vinyl chairs around the television, ready for the evening news.

I always enjoyed my shifts on Bluebell Ward. At the helm was an enthusiastic and motivated Ward Sister, whose leadership ensured the smooth operation of an organised and tidy ward environment. Sister Grove picked her team carefully, and she fostered a sense of professionalism and purpose that extended to every member. I noticed that the staff seemed empowered and valued under her guidance.

The hallmark of Bluebell Ward was its commitment to patient well-being and safety. I had a clinical placement there during my training, and the staff were commended for the standard of patient care in an environment characterised by dignity and respect. Good nursing care ensures that patients are adequately nourished, hydrated, and comfortable; maintaining their cleanliness, dryness, and warmth, and every aspect of care receives attention and dedication.

The low turnover rate among staff members was credited to Sister Grove's effective leadership. A cohesive team dynamic flourished under her guidance. The sense of inclusivity and mutual respect fostered an atmosphere where each team member felt appreciated. On Bluebell Ward, staff took every opportunity to make a meaningful difference in the lives of those entrusted to their care.

Excellence like this is rare.

Tonight, as I went about my duties, preparing to dispense the evening medications, a sudden yell from the male toilet area shattered the calm of the routine.

"Help!"

Startled, my senses sharpened, and I grabbed the drug trolley padlock and chain. My focus shifted to the urgent call for attention echoing through the ward.

Locking the trolley and slamming the clinic room door behind me, I raced towards the male toilet area. Reaching the male toilet area, I scanned the scene, looking for the source of the yell.

On the surface, I remained calm and composed, and my training and experience kicked in as I prepared to address whatever unexpected challenge might lay before me. Underneath, my heart was beating fast with anticipation and concern. With a mixture of relief and urgency, I quickly assessed the situation, ready to offer assistance and support to whoever needed It.

"Oi! Help! Help! Oh no! What are you doing?"

I quickly found where the shouting was coming from. Two nursing assistants were either side of Len in the toilet area. The three of them were jammed tightly inside the cubicle.

"What's happening?"

The younger nursing assistant looked at me guiltily.

"Um, it's…….. well, it's Len. His foot is stuck in the bog."

I stood on tiptoes, trying to catch a glimpse over their shoulders.

Despite the concern etched on the faces of the nursing assistants, there was a palpable tension tinged with amusement, evident in the way they bit their lips, struggling to contain their laughter.

Somehow, Len had managed to get his right foot into the toilet bowl and had pushed it halfway around the 's bend'. The water from the toilet was creeping slowly up his trousers. His foot was stuck fast.

"Have you tried pulling his leg out?"

"Yes," nodded the assistants, "we've done that. We've tried everything."

As Len stood in the toilet, a look of bewilderment on his face, the nursing assistants observed his movements with a mix of concern and anticipation. Len's jiggling and pushing of his leg mirrored the nervous energy in the cubicle, creating an atmosphere charged with uncertainty.

Suddenly, without warning, Len leaned forward and, with a swift motion, pushed the flush handle. A rush of water cascaded into the bowl, quickly overflowing and spilling onto the floor. The scene unfolded in a flurry of motion, catching us all off guard.

Caught on the hop by the unexpected deluge, we attempted to step back to avoid the rushing water, but our efforts were in vain. Our shoes were quickly soaked through, leaving us standing in a pool of water, grappling with the chaos unfolding before us.

In the confusion, Len remained unaware of the havoc he had caused, his actions driven by a moment of impulse and confusion. As the water continued to flow, we tried to work together to address the situation.

"Shit a brick!" bellowed Len. It was so loud and was such a strange thing for the former accountant to shout that it took everyone by surprise.

We glanced at each other and smirked, then started laughing. The more we tried not to laugh, the worse it got. Len was laughing too. We were all hanging on to each other laughing and squealing at the ridiculousness of the situation we were in. Len was laughing and coughing. Tears ran from his bright blue eyes and down his crinkled face. He jiggled and pumped his leg up and down, sloshing more water out of the bowl. He leant forwards again to push the flush. The three of us yelled "No!" in unison, laughing as we fielded his hand away from the flush.

"What shall we do, Claire?" one of them said, turning to me for guidance.

"I haven't a clue," I said so helplessly that it made us all crack up again.

Len pumped his leg with increasing vigour. We braced ourselves for the unexpected.

Suddenly, as if propelled by some unseen force, Len's foot shot out of his slipper with surprising power, dislodging it from the s-bend and causing him to lose his balance. Staggering backward, we caught him. Our quick reflexes prevented a potential fall. With a collective sigh of relief, we frog-marched Len out of the cubicle, our feet soaked and squelching.

In the dayroom, the other two staff looked up to see us heading back towards them. With tongue firmly planted in cheek, they quipped, "Having fun are we ladies?" The question dripped with sarcasm and good humour, and we all laughed.

After a cup of tea and a change of trousers and slippers, Len once again started his endless mooching around the ward.

The commotion in the toilet cubicle now behind me, with sodden shoes, I returned to the clinic room, unlocked the drugs trolley, wheeled it back into the day room, and prepared to start the medication round again.

Back to business....

My Diary

Shit a brick! Dear old Len. That was so funny today. I can still see his face. Old blue eyes. Shit a brick!

Us nurses have all got a similar dark and warped sense of humour. A warped sense goes a long way with some of the sad, serious, and shite situations we deal with.

It's often seen in high-stress jobs like the police, prison, and health services. A coping mechanism I reckon. A way of protecting ourselves against all that we see. I never laugh with anyone like I do with others from the hospital. We really get each other.

Decompressing and coping by cracking up laughing! Never at the expense of the patients. Always about what happened and what we saw and did.

I love having a good old giggle at The Fyshe talking about stuff over a drink. It helps to process it all. Johann's gonna love the one about Len. Shit a brick!

Laughing until we cry, shaking, and weeping with laughter. I love it. So, so good. Every story starts with "Do you remember that time, when...?"

It's unique. The ability us nurses have, to find humour in absurd situations. Good job we CAN find humour – no one ever asks how WE are! As long as the wards are staffed and nothing too bad happens, it all just ticks along. No questions asked. People come and go. The days roll into weeks and weeks roll into months and years. We are all just a number in the system.

8
THE GRAND SUMMER FETE

"It is not how much we give but how much love we put into giving."
Mother Teresa

St. Luke's wasn't just a healthcare facility—it was a big part of the local community with a cherished tradition of commemorating special days with the public.

Each year, the hospital organised a Grand Summer Fete, where staff, patients, families, and friends joined together to boost the patient comforts fund. Every stall and every activity raised funds earmarked for the enrichment of patients' lives.

From state-of-the-art televisions to the twinkling allure of Christmas decorations, every penny was used to uplift weary spirits. These gestures of kindness illuminated the wards with thoughtful presents for patients without families, vibrant art materials that ignited creative flames, and luxurious blankets to envelop the elderly with warmth. The annual fete wasn't merely a fundraising event; it was a celebration of the local community.

Months ahead of the annual fete, whispers of ideas began to circulate among the ward staff and their dedicated relatives. New ideas and plans took shape, sparking creativity and anticipation. With meticulous planning and boundless enthusiasm, each ward embarked on their quest to create the most captivating and enticing stall. Friendly ward rivalries bubbled to the surface, fuelling the determination to outshine the others and raise the most funds.

The Portering Team diligently assembled the stalls at the crack of dawn, transforming the green expanse in front of the hospital into a vibrant spectacle. A lively array of white canvas tents sprawled across the grass, adorned with cheerful rainbow bunting and whimsical homemade signs dangling from strings of balloons.

From traditional raffles to the whimsical challenge of a coconut shy, the fete boasted an array of stalls to entice visitors of all ages. The pick-a-straw stall beckoned with promises of hidden treasures, while the challenge to throw a ball into a jam jar to win a goldfish stirred excitement and laughter. Bric-a-brac treasures were unearthed, and racks of nearly new clothes offered hidden bargains waiting to be discovered. Amid the colourful array of offerings, the plant stall beckoned with verdant treasure. The fruit and vegetable stall brimmed with produce grown in the hospital gardens.

The delicious smell of hot dogs, burgers, fried onions, and freshly churned ice cream wafted from the nearby food vans. For those with a sweet tooth, candy floss spun into clouds of sugary delight.

Under the sheltering canopy of the tea tent, the Friends of St. Luke's extended warm hospitality, offering complimentary teas, coffees, and soft drinks to refresh and rejuvenate everyone. The aroma of baked cakes wafted from the cake stall, tempting passersby with irresistible treats.

In every corner, the air buzzed with laughter and chatter, and visitors revelled in the festive atmosphere. The annual Grand Summer Fete at St. Luke's Hospital was so much more than just an event—it was a celebration of community and tradition.

Children enjoyed face painting, queuing patiently to have their faces painted with the choice of butterflies and bees, a tiger face, or a clown.

The Nurse Managers coordinated various races such as running races, egg and spoon, and sack races. Each participant received a lollipop upon entry, and winners of first, second, and third place earned gold, silver, or bronze medals respectively, adorned with a blue lanyard inscribed with 'St. Luke's Grand Summer Fete'. The atmosphere was filled with cheering and laughter, and the competition remained light-hearted, ensuring that every child received recognition and a prize.

Staff who were on duty escorted patients from the wards to the fete in small groups, ensuring everyone had the opportunity to participate. Meanwhile, those enjoying their days off volunteered to manage the stalls, contributing their time and effort willingly and without compensation.

A spirit of goodwill permeated the event, as everyone embraced the opportunity to combine work and pleasure in support of a shared objective of enhancing the lives of patients. The prevailing attitude was one of positivity, blending enjoyment with a collective commitment to making a difference in the patients' experiences.

At the heart of the scene stood a raised platform encircled by the tents and stalls, serving as the focal point for the day's festivities. Here, a lively band struck up melodies, while the sound system reverberated with music and public announcements, infusing the air with an infectious energy that set the tone for a day of celebration and community spirit.

The 'band' comprised a diverse ensemble of patients and staff, united by their shared passion for music and performance. Meeting weekly to rehearse, they approached their performances with unwavering dedication and focus. Leading the group was Mrs. Pandora Page, a slender, tall figure with a pointed face and delicate half-spectacles. Clad in a traditional twinset and pearls, she epitomised both authority and warmth, instilling discipline with her strict yet kindly demeanour.

As the conductor, Mrs. Page approached her role with seriousness and precision, yet her gentle encouragement fostered an atmosphere of inclusivity and support. Within 'Pandora's Players,' there were no distinctions between staff or patients, all members were treated with equal respect and dignity.

When Mrs. Page lifted her baton, magic ensued as the ensemble harmonised in a medley of beloved tunes.

From the spirited strains of "When the Saints Go Marching In" to the nostalgic melodies of "Edelweiss" and "What a Wonderful World," the audience was transported on a musical journey. The infectious energy of "Yellow Submarine" and the timeless charm of "Daisy, Daisy" elicited smiles and sing-alongs broke out across the fete. With graceful movements of her baton, Mrs. Page invited participation from the audience with nods and encouraging smiles.

In her hands, music became a bridge that transcended barriers, uniting voices in song. 'Pandora's Players' filled the air with melody—they didn't just perform;

they shared moments of pure magic, leaving lasting memories for all who listened.

The pride exuded by the players was palpable and a demonstration of the transformative power of music. In a world where mental illness often chips away at one's sense of self and confidence, Pandora's Players found refuge and empowerment. Through a shared love of music, their spirits soared.

The journey with Pandora's Players was more than musical—the harmonious notes and synchronised rhythms helped to reclaim lost confidence. With each rehearsal and performance, barriers dissolved, and distinctions between staff and patients faded into insignificance.

During the afternoon, the music took centre stage, guided by the charismatic DJ Alastair, a staff nurse with a flair for entertainment. With a twinkle in his eye and a passion for music that rivalled professional DJs, Alastair introduced each number with infectious enthusiasm. Behind the turntables, he transformed into a whirlwind of energy, lost in the rhythm of the beats pulsating through his headphones. With every track, Alastair's face lit up with a grin that spoke volumes of his love for the music.

As the melodies filled the air, his contagious energy infused the crowd. Amidst the tunes and rhythms, he encouraged everyone to dance to the beat, and people found themselves bopping along.

This year, I was helping on the bric-a-brac stall. Tom and Lizzie also came along to help. It was something we all enjoyed doing. A real family affair.

The bric-a-brac stall was a mishmash of pots and pans, ornaments, trinkets, toys, games, books, glass vases, cutlery sets and bits of jewellery laid out on red and white checkered tablecloths.

The team were busy pricing each item and arranging them on the stall trestle tables. Most items were 50p or a pound.

Lizzie cast an eye over the children's toys. There was a rainbow-coloured bear with a red bow tied around its neck that looked familiar to her. She picked it up and inspected it closely.

"Hey Mum," she said, "I used to have one of these, didn't I?"

Guiltily, I muttered. "Erm, yes. Yes. You did…"

Lizzie saw that I was blushing. "Mum!! It's mine, isn't it?"

"Erm yes, yes, it was," I admitted, feeling a bit uncomfortable and embarrassed.

"Mum! You do this every year!"

"I know. You don't play with it, so I thought it could go to a good home and raise some money for the patients."

"Oh Mum. Really?"

"Do you want me to put it aside to take back home again?"

"No. It's alright. I don't mind. Have you sorted out any of my other stuff?"

Lizzie began to investigate each item.

"That Cluedo looks like ours! And that box of Lego! Mum! Really!!"

Tom was eyeing the toy cars. "Lizzie, half of these are mine!" He said, shaking his head and smiling. "I didn't even notice that they'd gone! What do you want us to do, Mum?" he asked, his voice eager with readiness to lend a hand.

I directed them to start arranging the toys and books, preparing them for the first customers. Smiling with pride, I watched my children dive into the task with enthusiasm. Their willingness to assist others less fortunate, happy to speak with people from all walks of life, filled my heart with warmth. I cherished the fact that they were unaffected by the stigma often associated with mental illness. Their natural empathy and openness allowed them to effortlessly engage with managers, porters, nurses, and patients, fostering connections that transcended labels and preconceptions.

Observing my children immersed in the bustling atmosphere of the fete, I wondered if either of them was destined to follow in my footsteps. Only time would reveal their future path.

I stepped away from manning the stall for half an hour and quickly made the rounds to look at all the other stalls, trying my hand at the pick-a-straw game, purchasing some raffle tickets, and exchanging greetings with everyone.

Afterwards, I bought a selection of homemade cakes to take home. The cake stall boasted a tempting selection of bakes from the hospital kitchen and home bakers from the wards. Meringues, fairy cakes, Swiss rolls, sausage rolls, jam tarts, scones, apple pies, cinnamon buns, currant buns, ginger snaps, chocolate cake, lemon drizzle, coffee and walnut slices, and chocolate crispy cakes adorned antique lace tablecloths, creating an inviting display.

I am not a baker. I really can't be bothered with the meticulous weighing of ingredients and precise timings required for baking cakes. I am proud to call myself a 'one-pot wonder chef' who prefers the simplicity of throwing everything together in a single pot.

My culinary expertise lies in dishes like curries, chillies, hot pots, stews, and soups. My 'chuck it all in' approach usually lends a deliciously spontaneous touch to my famous 'creations.'

But my unique cooking style, characterised by tossing in ingredients without measuring, means that I can never replicate any dish exactly.

My one-pot nights for friends are the stuff of legend, with flavours and aromas that lingered on tastebuds and in memories long after the gathering has ended.

My everyday cooking for the children often elicits a suspicious glance into the pot, accompanied by the inevitable question, 'What is it?'

Their query comes with a hint of trepidation, as they aren't always sure what culinary surprise awaits them.

When I got back to the bric-a-brac stall, I gave Tom and Lizzie their pocket money. They happily wandered off together to look around and see what they could spend their cash on.

The afternoon passed in a busy, happy blur. It was perfect weather, sunny, and warm. The Summer Fete was a highlight in everyone's calendar and a good opportunity to catch up with old friends and colleagues and arrange to meet up for a multi-generational fun family day out.

These were simple, fun times.

As the clock struck five, the last visitor bid farewell, and everyone pitched in for the cleanup.

Stalls and tents were dismantled, rubbish gathered, chairs stacked, and all equipment was carefully stowed away, awaiting the festivities of next year.

Each year, staff proclaimed the fete better than the last, and everyone looked forward to hearing about how much had been raised for the Patients Comfort Fund.

"St. Luke's News" was published monthly. The Occupational Therapy Department took on the responsibility of compiling and publishing the bulletin consistently each month. Patients were actively encouraged to contribute, and a small group, with the help of staff, edited each edition.

The A4 double-sided sheet provided brief updates on several topics such as new staff members, departures, weddings, and funerals within the St. Luke's community. Additionally, the bulletin featured news about promotions, hospital maintenance updates, ward outings, achievements by both staff and patients, fundraising initiatives, and upcoming events. Occasionally, there were engaging sections like quizzes or jokes, adding a light-hearted touch to the publication. The little newspaper served as a valuable resource, keeping everyone informed and fostering a sense of community within the hospital.

The highly anticipated issue following the fete reflected the community's collective effort and interest in the hospital's events and initiatives.

Everyone was keen to know how much was raised, comparing it to previous years, and to discover the plans for using the funds.

My Diary

Another fete done and dusted. I'm so proud of the kids. So willing to help. Tom got well stuck in clearing up. Poor Lizzie and her rainbow bear! While I think the fete is a good thing, I do think there should be more funding for patients' comfort. Some of the patients have no one. No one that shows up for them anyway. Not until they die – then all the relatives come creeping out of the woodwork looking for any money.

I'm glad Joe didn't turn up today. It's always a bit awkward if he does. Mum said she heard he's started seeing someone. Not sure how I feel about that. The kids haven't said anything. Good for Joe though. I wonder who she is?

9
MICHAEL

"It's so much darker when a light goes out than it would have been if it had never shone."
John Steinbeck

Maple Ward. Night Shift.
Acute Admission and Assessment Ward. Male. 25 beds.

Maple Ward catered to men experiencing severe episodes of mental illness or emotional distress who required immediate assessment, stabilization, and treatment. The goal was always to facilitate recovery and support their return to the community.

The men had complex presentations: acute psychosis or schizophrenia, often experiencing severe hallucinations, delusions, or disordered thinking. Some had severe depression, anxiety, or other mood disorders, and many were at risk of harming themselves or others. They may have recently attempted suicide, had a history of self-harm, or struggled with severe substance use disorders requiring detoxification and rehabilitation. Balancing the needs of such a variety of patients—those with personality disorders, acute stress disorders, psychosis, or manic episodes associated with bipolar disorder—made working there very challenging at times.

Sister Jeffreys, the nurse in charge, was renowned for her unwavering strictness. Staff wore "mufti" on the admission wards, meaning their own smart but casual clothing. Sister Jeffreys upheld the standards of behavior and dress instilled in her during her nurse training in the 1950s. She was a vigilant presence, sitting in the office awaiting the arrival of each staff member for their shift handover. Unfamiliar staff and students were warned of her high standards, and any who chose to ignore the warnings did so at their peril. She looked each person up and down, from head to toe and back again, and any nurse who dared to arrive inappropriately dressed for duty on the acute ward faced her wrath. Peering sternly from behind her thick NHS-issue glasses, Sister Jeffreys would firmly declare, *"No armpits, knees, or cleavage on show, nurse! Go home and change NOW!"* Her words left no room for negotiation, ensuring that professionalism and propriety were always maintained on the ward.

Maple Ward ran with a standard minimum staffing for night duty: two trained staff members and one nursing assistant. This staffing model was common in many healthcare settings to ensure adequate coverage and support during nighttime hours when patient needs might still require attention.

The rotation of staff between day and night duty was standard practice, allowing staff to gain experience and exposure to different shifts while also ensuring that workload and responsibilities were distributed fairly among team members. (*9) The three-month rotation of day duty followed by one month of night duty helped prevent burnout and allowed staff members to adapt to different schedules and routines. It also ensured continuity of care for patients, as staff rotated through different shifts and became familiar with patients' needs and routines regardless of the time of day. I didn't mind working the night shift because I knew I could sleep well at home during the day while the children were at school or at Joe's. A big positive for me was that the hours attracted better pay.

Maple Ward was set for a relatively quiet night with several beds vacant and some patients on overnight leave. The atmosphere was calm, and the remaining patients were engaged in watching TV, chatting, and enjoying a nighttime drink and biscuits. The nightly routine of taking medication and then watching the ten o'clock news helped to create a sense of structure and familiarity for the patients, and there was a relaxed, cosy atmosphere on the ward. Patients drifted off to bed after the evening activities and began to settle down comfortably for the night. The relatively low patient occupancy and the peaceful atmosphere helped us to provide attentive care. There was time to chat and offer reassurance, ensuring the patients' comfort and safety while also maintaining a sense of normalcy and routine.

By 11 o'clock, the dormitory was quiet, and the men were all sleeping. I was on duty with Dave, a Senior Staff Nurse, and Maureen, an experienced nursing assistant. Together, we were a well-balanced team, providing expertise and experience. I'd enjoyed the previous night shifts we'd worked together. We worked well as a team and efficiently completed the tasks necessary for patient care with ease, effective communication, and collaboration. We each pottered around with a sense of purpose and productivity, attending to our various duties and responsibilities.

I wore my own sort of uniform. An outfit of black trousers and black Doc Marten shoes with a simple blouse or plain jumper. I kept a set of clothes just for work. It was easier that way.

At 11:30 p.m., we plonked ourselves in the three chairs that Maureen had moved near the door of the dormitory. She'd prepared a tea tray, and we enjoyed a relaxed cuppa together, talking quietly in the semi-darkened room. More than an hour passed in amicable chat and comfortable silence. We exchanged the newspaper between us, talking quietly, sharing the stories, opinions, and snippets of news that caught our attention. The atmosphere was one of companionship and mutual respect, and our words and silence intermingled seamlessly. There was a sense of understanding and connection between us.

In the quiet of the dormitory, we took turns checking on the patients every thirty minutes or so, ensuring their safety and well-being. Just one patient was assigned Level 3 observations, with the remaining patients on Level 4 observations. (*10) Walking softly among the rows of sleeping men, we gently monitored the patients, confirming their peaceful slumber and steady breathing. After completing each round, we returned to our chairs, signaling with a nod or a thumbs up to indicate that all was well. With a sense of duty fulfilled, we recorded their observations on the check chart before settling back into our seats, resuming our vigil in the tranquil night.

At 2:30 a.m., the ward office telephone rang. "Here we go," said Dave as he headed to the office. Maureen and I exchanged a knowing glance, a silent acknowledgment passing between us. There was a sense of anticipation and a feeling that something significant was about to unfold. Perhaps it was a subtle shift in atmosphere, or our intuition honed by our shared experiences. Whatever it was, we felt it keenly and braced ourselves for the impending event, whatever it might be.

After about ten minutes, Dave appeared from the office, breaking the stillness with his announcement. His words confirmed our premonition that something was about to happen. An admission was imminent: a man, aged sixty, with no prior psychiatric history, was being admitted, possibly under a section.

The news carried weight and injected a sense of urgency into the atmosphere. Maureen and I exchanged another glance, then sprang into action. The unexpected arrival of a patient under such circumstances demanded immediate attention and care, prompting us to prepare for his arrival and any challenges that might lay ahead. We tidied up the chairs and tea table, clearing the space to accommodate the new admission. In the single side room, we checked that the bed was made with fresh, clean linen, then turned our attention to the administrative tasks, gathering the admission forms and folder in the interview room. Organising the necessary documentation in advance streamlined the admission process and ensured that all essential information would be readily available for the patient's arrival.

As we busied ourselves with preparations, Dave shared the information he had received about the incoming patient. His tone conveyed concern, as he relayed the details to us, ensuring we were prepared for what lay ahead. As Dave shared the details, the gravity of the situation became clear. The circumstances surrounding the admission painted a concerning picture, and I felt empathy for him, recognising the profound anguish he must be feeling.

Neighbours had raised concerns about the man with the police after noticing a foul smell coming from his flat. They knew his mother had died recently, but no one remembered seeing him since. The neighbors' growing concern stemmed not only from the foul smell but also from the man's increasingly erratic behavior. Movement, talking, and shouting had been heard from inside the flat at all hours, raising red flags about his well-being and state of mind. Reports of him talking gibberish to himself, singing loudly, and creating disturbances by banging pots and pans together gave a distressing picture of his deteriorating mental state. Their observations hinted at a potentially complex and challenging situation, underlining the importance of a careful and sensitive approach.

When the police arrived, the young constable who had been tasked with an initial assessment tried to talk to the man through the door. Realising he needed help; he consulted the on-call mental health team and waited for backup to arrive. It took an hour for a social worker, a psychiatrist, and two more uniformed police officers to reach the flat. The man's refusal to engage or allow entry, coupled with the overpowering smell emanating from his flat, painted a bleak picture of his condition. His distress was obvious, evidenced by his pacing, sobbing, and muttering, which emphasised the severity of the situation. The scene unfolding behind the closed door spoke volumes about the man's internal turmoil and the depth of his suffering.

The social worker approached the door cautiously, mindful of the delicate nature of the situation. Through the thin barrier, they could hear the muffled sobs of a man in distress, his anguish palpable even from outside.

"We're here to help you, sir," the social worker called out. "You're not alone."

The man's response was a harrowing plea tinged with despair.

"Just leave me be... I can't take it anymore. Life's not worth living. I'd rather be dead."

The psychiatrist exchanged a knowing glance with the social worker, their shared understanding an indication of years spent navigating human suffering.

As negotiations faltered and tensions mounted, the decision weighed heavily upon them. There was no further response from inside the flat. All attempts at communication were now met with silence. With a solemn nod, the police prepared to execute the final option: breaching the door.

"Stand away from the door," called the police officers, "we're coming in."

The sound of splintering wood filled the air, and the police pushed inside, finding the man crouched in the hallway, hands covering his head, his eyes hollow with despair, his spirit battered by the weight of unseen burdens.

The scene was one of utter neglect and decay, grim evidence of the depths of despair that had consumed its inhabitant. The tableau of filth, squalor, and neglect that met the responders defied comprehension. The kitchen lay desolate, covered with a blanket of rubbish. Newspapers littered the floor, their faded headlines, a sad reflection of a world left behind. Piles of unwashed plates teetered precariously, their surfaces obscured by the creeping tendrils of mold and decay. Flies buzzed lazily in the stagnant air, their incessant hum adding to the macabre atmosphere.

In the bedroom, the carpets squelched beneath their feet, sodden and oozing with the weight of accumulated filth. The bed was buried beneath layers of filthy duvets and soiled clothing. Neglect was evident on every surface. The lounge was buried beneath a mountain of refuse. Cardboard boxes, magazines, and discarded electronics jostled for space amidst the detritus of a life left in ruins. Dust and dirt clung to every surface like a shroud, evidence of time passing in isolation and neglect.

As they surveyed the scene before them, the responders were struck by the enormity of the task ahead and the poor, desperate soul in need of help. A veritable sea of bottles, boxes, and tins covered every worktop, table, and bookcase. Each container was filled with a noxious concoction of fluids ranging from pale yellow to deep brown. A sickening realisation began to dawn. Every container, once an innocent vessel of sustenance, now harboured a sinister secret. Urine and faeces lay cradled within their confines. Many of the containers bore lids, their contents concealed from prying eyes. Others were covered with tin foil or cling film, their makeshift seals a feeble attempt to contain the stench that now engulfed them. Plastic bags, neatly tied at the top, served as vessels for the noxious brew within. Every cupboard, every nook and cranny of the flat, was filled with the hoarder's obsession. Even the oven, once a symbol of nourishment and warmth, now lay dormant beneath the weight of the odorous, rancid vessels that crowded its confines.

As they stood amidst the wreckage, the responders could scarcely believe their eyes. This was no mere hoarder's den; it was a demonstration of how despair could consume even the most resilient of souls.

Michael stood before them, trembling amidst the chaos of his kitchen, his fragile frame quivering with each ragged breath. His once vibrant eyes were now hollow, haunted by his situation. His small, wiry figure appeared lost in the sea of his despair, his long gray hair straggling like wisps of smoke around his pallid face. Bald patches dotted his scalp, his skin dry and flaky. Clad in an oversized black jumper, baggy corduroy trousers, and green Wellington boots, he was alone and adrift in a world that seemed to have forgotten him. With trembling hands, he clutched at his face and hair, his movements frantic and disjointed. His jumper, once a shield against the cold, now hung limply from his emaciated frame, a tattered remnant of a life left in ruins.

"It was me," he muttered, his voice a plaintive whisper lost amidst the cacophony of his own torment. "I need new clothes. It was me. I've hurt my nose."

The skin on his face was a patchwork of scars and scratches. Yellow and green pimples marred his nose, their oozing wounds festering and decaying beneath the surface. His lips, cracked and parched, bore the ravages of neglect, while his teeth, yellowed and uneven, betrayed a life spent in the shadows.

It was a pitiful sight, a heartbreaking tableau of human suffering laid bare for all to see. In Michael's eyes, the responders saw his pain.

"It was me. I need new clothes. It was me. I've hurt my nose," he muttered repeatedly.

The social worker approached Michael with gentle reassurance, her voice soothing and quiet against the storm of his emotions. With practiced ease, she navigated a delicate dance of persuasion, each word chosen with care to build trust and instill hope. With patience and compassion, she gently offered him a lifeline amidst the chaos that surrounded them.

She spoke quietly of the hospital as a place of refuge, a sanctuary where he could find solace and support during his struggles.

Just as they neared the precipice of acceptance, Michael's resolve wavered, his fragile grip on hope slipping through his fingers. With each step forward, he hesitated, his eyes clouded with doubt and fear.

"It was me," he whispered, his voice trembling with uncertainty. "I need new clothes. It was me. I've hurt my nose."

The social worker nodded, understanding that Michael's deep grief at the loss of his mother meant his healing would likely be fraught with setbacks and obstacles. She stood by his side, offering him the space to find his own way. She reassured him that she would be there for him and continued with gentle persistence until he found the courage to take the ultimate step and agree to a voluntary admission to the hospital.

The psychiatrist, weary from the late-night call and eager to return to the comfort of his own bed, felt a twinge of impatience as the negotiation with Michael wore on. His professional demeanor strained against the exhaustion, that gnawed at his resolve.

"Okay, he's coming in. I don't think we need to section him," he declared, his words tinged with a hint of relief.

Turning his attention to Michael, he cut through the uncertainty firmly. "So, you're coming into St. Luke's then, Michael," he stated, his tone leaving little room for negotiation.

Suddenly, realising the gravity of the situation, Michael nodded in reluctant agreement. The choice had been made for him, it was clear, even if it felt like a surrender to forces beyond his control.

"Jolly good show, mate," said the psychiatrist, his fatigue momentarily forgotten. With a brisk nod to the social worker and police, he made a quick exit, saying he would catch up with the ward staff in the morning. The promise of rest beckoned like a beacon in the night, and he set off before the plans could change.

Michael, escorted by the social worker, walked hesitantly down the stairs to the waiting ambulance, muttering, "It was me. I need new clothes. It was me. I've hurt my nose." He repeated it over and over, his voice a fragile echo of his turmoil.

We stood at the ward doors, waiting to receive Michael as the ambulance pulled up in the early hours of the morning. The fluorescent lights cast stark shadows against the sterile walls, lending an air of solemnity to the scene.

Wrapped in a blanket, Michael emerged from the ambulance, his small frame shrouded in uncertainty. His eyes darted nervously from side to side as he followed the social worker, police officer, and paramedic through the doors. With minimal conversation, the police officer and paramedic took their leave, seamlessly handing Michael into our care.

As the doors closed behind them, Michael stood in the sterile hallway, his gaze fixed suspiciously on the uncertain horizon before him.

Maureen, with her compassionate nature, stepped forward to offer him a cup of tea. Wrapping her arm around his bony shoulders, ignoring the stench emanating from his body, hair, breath, and clothing, she murmured softly, "You'd like that, wouldn't you? You look very tired. Come with me now, and let's get you sorted. Now, what did you say your name was?" she asked gently, as she guided him towards the admissions room, her voice a small sign of hope in the darkness that threatened to engulf him.

"Michael... I'm Michael," he replied, his voice trembling with emotion. "It was me. I need new clothes. It was me. I've hurt my nose," he repeated, this time softer, like a mantra of his suffering.

The social worker shared the few details she had gathered about Michael with Dave and me. She resolved to begin the process of locating his GP, reaching out to any known relatives or friends, and gathering comprehensive information about his background, including potential benefit claims. The absence of a documented mental health history seemed unusual given Michael's current state, prompting a deeper investigation into his circumstances. She promised Michael she would maintain close communication throughout his admission and assessment process and pledged to facilitate any necessary arrangements upon his eventual discharge.

As we speculated about the circumstances surrounding Michael's admission, I took charge of the admission pack and moved ahead toward the interview room. Meanwhile, Dave diligently conducted the thirty-minute checks on the other patients. Years of experience grant good nurses a communication style that demands few words. Seasoned nurses develop an intuitive understanding of their role and quickly discern whether they're working alongside another experienced nurse they can trust. We can recognise a dependable clinician a mile away. It's a sort of sixth sense.

Michael sat at the dining room table, sipping tea with Maureen. The simple act of consuming a mug of tea and four digestive biscuits seemed to ease his tension. He appeared visibly more relaxed.

When I asked him to follow me into the interview room, a flicker of apprehension danced in his eyes. Glancing suspiciously at Maureen, he whispered again, "It was me. I need new clothes. It was me. I've hurt my nose." His right leg trembled with nerves, and his hands clutched the mug tightly as if seeking comfort in its warmth.

"Everything's okay," I assured Michael calmly. "We'll handle the paperwork for your admission together, right here."

I sat beside him and placed the forms on the table, making sure he could see everything clearly. With a steady hand, I found my pen and began filling in the necessary details, starting with "Michael" on the line marked "First name."

"What's your surname, Michael?" I asked.

Michael looked down at the forms and said nothing. He stared at them for some time, taking furtive glances over his shoulder, shaking his head as if responding to someone else.

"If I give you the pen, would you like to fill in the form?"

He shook his head and continued avoiding eye contact, staring bleakly downward.

As I settled beside him, Maureen discreetly excused herself and checked in with Dave to ensure there were no outstanding tasks that needed her help. While she attended to the sleeping men in the dormitory, conducting regular observations and tidying away linen and towels, she also kept a vigilant watch from afar, monitoring Michael's interaction with me.

Maureen was wonderful to work with. She was a safe pair of hands, dedicated to her role, and made genuine efforts to approach patients with compassion, empathy, and understanding. I really liked her. She understood the importance of fostering a relationship in an environment of acceptance and support, making patients feel valued and respected amidst their mental health struggles. Patients warmed to her easily. Her openness and sense of humor helped them trust her. She never spoke down to them, and she tried to do what she promised. She was as honest with them as she could be.

Maureen made her way to the sluice room with a bag of linen, pausing as she passed by.

"How are you getting on, Michael? Need any help?" she asked, her voice laced with genuine concern.

Michael looked up and shook his head, saying that he was managing well for the moment.

"Honestly, the amount of paperwork they must do these days! I hope you're giving Claire all the info she needs. I don't want her to get in trouble with the big boss if she hasn't completed the paperwork properly. There's a lot to do, and we'll be going home soon," she teased lightly before continuing on her way.

"Jones," said Michael quietly.

I smiled at him. "Surname: Jones. Thank you, Mr. Jones,".

Maureen's intervention had been helpful.

With some prompting from me, Michael and I completed the admission form together. Seeing that things were progressing well, Maureen winked as she bustled past us on her way to the office.

Michael explained that his mother had passed away nearly a year ago. He had been caring for her at home. They had no other relatives, and it had been just the two of them for years. Once the funeral was over, he began to worry that he would die too and somehow believed he had caused her death.

Overwhelmed with grief and loneliness, he said he decided to sacrifice his sleep, staying awake all night, waiting for a knock at the door, a phone call, or a visit from the authorities. As the days passed, he continued to deprive himself of sleep, relying on caffeine and energy drinks to stay awake. The exhaustion and stress mounted. One night, after several days of sleeplessness, he began to experience hallucinations. He heard voices whispering his name and saw strange shadows moving around the room. He thought it was his mother coming to see him. He missed her terribly and became paranoid, convinced she was watching him.

Becoming increasingly agitated he began to have delusional thoughts, convinced that he was being watched and that his neighbours were plotting against him. (*11) As we talked, Michael began to relax. He yawned, his head nodding as the weight of exhaustion finally caught up with him. By the time the day staff arrived for their early shift, he was tucked up in bed, still in his clothes but calm enough to allow sleep to welcome him.

After a thorough evaluation and assessment process over the next three weeks, Michael was diagnosed with first-episode psychosis, caused by grief and sleep deprivation.

The next time I was rostered to work on Maple Ward a few weeks later, I was surprised and delighted to see Michael looking so much better.

He greeted me with a smile. "Hello there! You're the nurse who admitted me, aren't you?" he said, then went on to update me on his medication and treatment. I could see he had developed a keen awareness of his current mental state and was openly acknowledging his deep grief since the loss of his mother. He said he felt embarrassed about how he had spiraled out of control. Despite his struggles, he seemed thoughtful and articulate. Laughing, he shook his head in wonder, trying to grasp how things had gotten so bad. He had had time to reflect and now recognized how his circumstances had unfolded, a combination of grief, lack of sleep, and paranoia.

Talking to him, I realised that his ability to acknowledge and reflect so clearly on everything was a crucial step in his journey toward healing and recovery. He thanked me again for my support on the night of his admission, and his gratitude was so genuine that I felt a bit emotional. I was hopeful for his future after seeing his progress. Moments like these reaffirm a nurse's dedication to their career. It's a tough job, but one that can truly make a difference.

My Diary

Wowzers. That chap (M) admitted three weeks ago in the middle of the night with psychosis is so much better! I didn't think he would come out of that so quickly! He's gone from not knowing who he is to almost being ready to go home. Maureen said he's quite an educated bloke. He looks so much better after some food, a bath, and a haircut. Strange what grief and loneliness can do to you. He is one of our rare success stories. Good to see. It was nice that he recognised me. I hardly recognised him! I felt touched when he thanked me. Almost tearful. He must be so lonely without his mum. I don't think he has any other family. Poor chap.

10
SID SULLIVAN

"Life is short, and it's up to you to make it sweet."
Sadie Delany

Sid Sullivan was a charismatic figure with a larger-than-life personality and a knack for selling an eclectic array of goods. An ex-nurse, now long retired, he was the go-to guy for anything we might need, from perfume to clothing, from radios to cup-a-soup. Sid was a beloved presence, brightening up the nighttime atmosphere of the hospital wards.

His visits were eagerly anticipated by all the staff on duty. He came every couple of weeks, arriving perfectly on time for our midnight break. With his trusty suitcase in tow, Sid made his entrance, calling out in his booming voice, "Come on now, ladies and gentlemen, come on girls and boys! See what treasures old Sid has for you today!"

His sales pitch was as charming as it was effective, and we would gather around, eager to peruse his wares. He had a way of making everyone feel special, whether we were buying something or simply enjoying his company and a rummage through his goods.

In an era before charity shops became commonplace, Sid filled a unique role in our hospital community. He wasn't only a merchant; he was a friend, bringing a bit of joy and excitement with him.

The mystery of where he sourced his goods only added to his allure. Despite the curiosity of those around him, he kept a strict policy of secrecy, repeating his mantra, "Ask no questions, and I'll tell you no lies." His reassurance that everything was "legal and above-board" did little to quell our speculation, but the quality of his goods kept us coming back for more.

With a flair for the dramatic, Sid would unveil the treasures in his suitcase with a flourish, enticing us with promises of bargains and delights. Each visit brought a new assortment of goods, carefully curated to appeal to us, his valued customers.

Tonight, it was scents and underwear. He had an eye for the finer things in life, offering luxury packs of three pairs of knickers in an array of colors, each delicately edged with lace. It was this attention to detail and his ability to cater to our desires that made Sid a legend in the hospital. The air was filled with the scent of exotic perfumes and aftershaves, transporting us to far-off lands with just a squirt and a sniff. Perfumes like Youth Dew, Rive Gauche, Shalimar, Tweed, Anais Anais, and Eden, and classic aftershaves like Old Spice, English Leather, and Brut, filled the air with their intoxicating fragrances.

As we indulged in our impromptu midnight shopping spree, spraying perfume and admiring the luxurious underwear, the atmosphere was light and jovial. Sid, true to form, made a tidy profit that night, his charisma and charm working their magic as usual.

The mood took a slight turn when Angie later made an unexpected discovery about her purchase. Sid had already left the hospital when, with a mixture of surprise and frustration, she realised that the knickers she had bought were flawed—the side seam had been sewn together upside down, causing them to be perpetually twisted.

"Oi!" Angie exclaimed, drawing attention to her predicament. "Sid's sold me a duff pair of pants! They're twisted!"

We gathered around to inspect the faulty garment, our amusement growing as we examined Angie's purchase, passing it between us and smirking. We hastily checked our own packs, relieved to find they were free of any defects.

"You've always got your knickers in a twist, Ange. That's why Sid sold you that pair!" someone quipped, prompting laughter from the group.

"Don't get your knickers in a knot, Ange, Sid'll give you a new pack," another chimed in, earning a round of chuckles.

Angie took the teasing and ribbing from us in good humor, and her laughter rang out in response to our playful jabs. "Knowing my luck, this time all three will be twisted!" Angie retorted with a grin, her playful spirit undiminished. With a mischievous glint in her eye, she turned the situation on its head—quite literally. Ignoring our teasing, she grabbed the twisted knickers and, with a playful flourish, slipped them over her head, positioning her face comically within the leg holes. She paraded around with the knickers perched on her head, her infectious laughter filling the room. Embracing the banter with good spirit, she reveled in the attention and our uproarious laughter.

Despite the mystery surrounding his goods, one thing was certain: Sid Sullivan knew how to bring a touch of glamour and excitement to the often-mundane world of hospital life.

And for that, he would always be fondly remembered.

11
BRIAN

"Holding on to anger is like grasping a hot coal with the intent of throwing it at someone else; you are the one who gets burned."
Buddha

Aspen Ward. Day Shift.
Admission and assessment ward. Mixed sex. 22 beds.

I was on a day shift working nine to five, and I had been tasked with providing close observation for Brian, who had been admitted to Aspen Ward after a harrowing suicide attempt. For some reason, the gravity of his circumstances weighed heavily upon me as I embarked on my duties. I was acutely aware of the fragility of life and the profound pain that often accompanies such desperate acts.

Brian's world had been shattered when his wife told him she wanted a divorce. He struggled to understand, let alone accept her decision. The rupture of their relationship left him reeling, and his mind was consumed by a tempest of disbelief and anguish. Despite his pleas, she remained adamant. In his despair, Brian saw no way forward other than the path of suicide.

The details surrounding his suicide attempt painted a chilling picture of meticulous planning and tragic timing. In his despair, he orchestrated a calculated and massive overdose, combining prescribed medication with over-the-counter drugs and alcohol, with the absolute intention of ending his life.

Believing that his wife would be away for the weekend visiting her mother, he took the opportunity to carry out his plan without fear of interruption. He meticulously timed his actions, ensuring he would not be discovered until it was too late to intervene.

But fate interfered in the form of a seemingly mundane detail—a forgotten jar of local honey. As Brian's wife left for her mother's house, she inadvertently left behind the honey and had to return to collect it just an hour after her departure. It was this small, unforeseen delay that proved to be the difference between life and death for Brian.

Had she *not* returned for it, Brian's lifeless body would have remained undiscovered until her planned return on Sunday evening. The grim reality of his death would have been etched in the silent stillness of their home, leaving behind a haunting vignette of the depths of his despair and the tragic finality of his actions.

Fate had other plans, and her return thwarted his carefully laid scheme, offering him a reprieve from the brink of oblivion. This near miss was a stark reminder of the unpredictable twists and turns that shape our existence.

As Brian grappled with humiliation in the aftermath of his failed attempt, he was forced to confront the glaring reality of his circumstances and the depths of his pain.

The task of providing close observation for Brian extended beyond mere surveillance. It forced me to bear witness to the depths of his despair and attempt to offer a glimmer of hope in the face of seemingly insurmountable odds. I tried to tune into the subtle shifts in his behavior, watching for signs of distress or danger. It was tiring sitting with him—his demeanor spoke volumes. His sullen silence and brooding presence cast a heavy pall over the atmosphere in the small side room. It was as though an invisible storm raged within him, his anger simmering just beneath the surface. I could feel it, hanging in the air like a thick, suffocating fog.

I found myself navigating the tense silence enveloping Brian. He refused to engage in conversation. Despite my best efforts to reach out and offer support, he remained aloof and withdrawn, retreating into sleep as a means of escaping the turmoil of his own thoughts. The depths of his despair seemed insurmountable.

In the confines of Aspen Ward, staff gently tried to forge a connection, offering a lifeline to connect him to the realm of the living. With kind words and compassionate gestures, we tried to break through the walls of his despair, offering support in his darkest hour.

The Level One observation persisted relentlessly—an unyielding vigil stretching on for twenty-four hours a day for over two grueling weeks. Brian found himself ensnared in a web of constant scrutiny, his every move watched, and his every word dissected under the unrelenting gaze of those tasked with his care.

Day after day, he was subjected to the probing inquiries of psychiatrists, each interview another reminder of the torment gripping his soul. And with each passing session, his same grim refrain echoed through the sterile confines of the consultation room. Avoiding eye contact, he repeated, "I wish my suicide attempt had been successful. I do not wish to live. If I could, I would try again."

The words were uttered with chilling conviction and painted a bleak portrait of his state of mind, like a landscape ravaged by the relentless onslaught of despair and hopelessness. Despite our best efforts to offer consolation and support, his resolve remained unyielding, his desire for escape eclipsing any hope for a brighter tomorrow.

Each encounter with Brian served as a sobering reminder of the fragility of the human spirit and the iron grip of mental illness. I found it frustrating and sad. I felt that I had used all the tools I had in my toolkit, but nothing made a difference.

Despite our team's efforts to offer him comfort and help, we found ourselves grappling with the stark reality of his suffering and the futility of our interventions. We were confronted with the harsh truth that some wounds run too deep to be healed with mere words or gestures. It was like talking to a brick wall.

Yet we refused to give up hope, knowing that even in despair, there often existed the potential for redemption and renewal. We pressed on, and even though at times our resolve wavered, we were determined to support him as he navigated the treacherous terrain of his own inner turmoil.

As the days within the confines of Aspen Ward wore on, a subtle but unmistakable shift began to take hold within Brian. Like a flickering ember reigniting into flame, a tiny glimmer of transformation appeared—a gradual thawing of the icy grip encasing his heart.

The anger that simmered beneath the surface was slowly softening, a gradual dissipation of the storm clouds that had shrouded his soul. The air around him seemed lighter, infused with a newfound sense of calm. Brian slowly relinquished the weight of his grievances and bitterness towards his wife and allowed himself to embrace the possibility of healing.

Where once silence reigned supreme, there was now an openness, a willingness to share the burden of his pain with those of us who looked to understand.

With each passing interaction, Brian's voice appeared to grow stronger, his words imbued with a newfound clarity and conviction. The shadows of doubt began to recede, replaced by the dawning light of optimism and hope. Where once he had spoken of death as a release, now he dared to entertain the prospect of a fresh start and began talking about the possibility of moving to be near his sister and her family.

In his journey toward healing, Brian was thankful for the support of his sister in Scotland, calling her a beacon of love and hope in his darkest hours. Despite the distance separating them, she visited him twice, her presence a comforting reminder of the familial bonds that transcended their physical distance.

She telephoned him every day, her voice a lifeline connecting him to the world beyond the sterile confines of Aspen Ward. With every conversation, she infused his spirit with words of encouragement and reassurance for the future.

In a tangible display of her devotion, she sent cards and small gifts imbued with warmth and affection as a reminder of her love. She shared details of houses and flats in her neighborhood, offering him a glimpse of a new future life filled with possibility and promise.

With the days turning into weeks and the weeks into months, a gradual transformation unfolded within Brian. He began to emerge from the depths of his anguish, his spirit buoyed by the steady tide of progress and healing. With each passing day, Brian's condition improved, his once-pervasive despair giving way to a newfound sense of hope and resilience. The watchful eyes of the medical and nursing teams noted his progress with cautious optimism, their steadfast support an inspiration on his journey toward recovery.

As his mental state stabilised and his symptoms abated, Brian's observation levels on the ward gradually decreased, showing the gains he made in reclaiming control over his own well-being.

After five long months of dedicated effort and determination, Brian reached a significant milestone in his recovery journey. With the support of the hospital staff, he was granted the privilege of short, supervised walks around the hospital grounds, each step showing the progress he made and the resilience of the human spirit. With each walk, he told staff he could feel the weight of his burdens slowly lifting, replaced by a sense of hope that he thought was long gone.

Brian's road to recovery continued to unfold, and the supervised walks around the hospital grounds became a cherished ritual. They were a daily reprieve from the confines of his former solitude. With each passing day, the duration of the walks stretched, extending to a full hour out under the watchful gaze of the hospital staff.

The benefits of these daily excursions were readily apparent, both to Brian and those who bore witness to his transformation.

Brian's progress continued unabated, his strides growing ever more confident as he moved boldly toward a new future of possibilities living near his sister.

Six months into his admission to Aspen Ward, his progress continued to astound those who witnessed his journey from despair to hope. With each passing day, he appeared to blossom further, his once-shrouded spirit now infused with a newfound vitality and purpose. He talked about his plans for the move and showed the staff estate agent pictures of possible new housing.

Brian embarked on short, solitary walks around the hospital grounds, chatting warmly with the porters, staff, visitors, and patients as he did so. He immersed himself in the diverse array of groups and activities offered at the Day Centre. From the therapeutic embrace of art therapy to the culinary delights of cooking skills classes, he took every opportunity, seeming eager to explore the possibilities that lay before him.

As night descended upon Aspen Ward, staff saw Brian in restful slumber, his mind appearing at peace and his spirit buoyed by the promise of a brighter tomorrow.

His journey towards recovery progressed, and his commitment to his treatment plan remained steadfast. Each day, he attended the Day Centre, eager to take part in the activities and interactions that had become an integral part of his healing process. He continued to take short walks in the hospital grounds, relishing the opportunity to connect with nature and enjoy the serenity of his surroundings.

He had a renewed sense of purpose, and his confidence in his ability to navigate the world outside the confines of Aspen Ward grew stronger with each passing day. He remained vigilant in adhering to the agreed-upon times for his return to the ward, understanding the importance of structure and routine as he worked towards his goal of discharge.

Behind the scenes, Brian's discharge plan was meticulously crafted and documented. Every detail had been carefully considered, from the timing of his sister's arrival to the arrangements for his transport back to her hometown in Scotland, where he would begin his new life. It seemed that everything was falling into place.

Or so it seemed....

A week before his scheduled discharge, Brian did not return to Aspen Ward for lunch as planned.

I happened to be on duty that morning, responsible for completing the lunchtime register of patients. As I checked the patients off, I realised that our steadfast Brian—whose punctuality had become a hallmark of his presence—was conspicuously absent. At first, I assumed he might have opted to have lunch at the Day Centre, a deviation from his usual routine but not entirely unheard of. However, as the moments stretched into minutes and Brian did not materialise, my concern began to mount.

I alerted the nurse in charge and called the Day Centre, who confirmed that Brian had left and headed back to the ward thirty minutes earlier. The sinking feeling in my stomach deepened, and my mind raced with troubling possibilities. Something was wrong.

Brian's absence sent internal alarm bells ringing through the team. In the last six weeks, he had never once deviated from his routine, always arriving on time and adhering to the agreed-upon schedule without fail. His sudden disappearance from this pattern sent ripples of worry through us, prompting immediate action to search for him.

The nurse in charge informed the duty nurse manager that Brian was missing, and two staff members from Aspen Ward were dispatched to search the hospital grounds, leaving me and another nursing assistant to continue serving lunch and ensure the safety of the other patients.

Brian was nowhere to be found within the hospital grounds. The porter, however, mentioned he thought he had seen a man fitting Brian's description walking out of the main gates as he drove in to work.

In a fortunate stroke of timing, Jason, one of our nursing assistants, had his car keys with him. Recognising the urgency of the situation, he wasted no time springing into action. He quickly told the porter to telephone us on Aspen Ward to let us know he was driving down to the nearby village to search for Brian.

These were the days before mobile phones, making communication more challenging. Jason's resourcefulness ensured that we remained informed as he hurriedly made his way to his car, ready to search for our missing patient.

The road from St. Luke's led down to the nearby village, with its pub, corner shop, post office, church, and railway station.

Jason drove quickly, eyes fixed on the road ahead, his sense of foreboding growing with every passing second. As he neared the railway station, he spotted a police car parked near the crossing, blue lights flashing. The barrier gates remained down, and police were redirecting traffic away from the station.

His stomach dropped.

Jason quickly abandoned his car in a gateway and approached the police officer directing traffic. Flashing his hospital badge, he explained who he was and asked if anything had happened. The police officer confirmed there had been a fatality on the train tracks. Someone had jumped in front of a train.

Jason's heart sank. Deep down, he sensed that this had something to do with Brian.

He knocked on the door of a nearby house, explaining the situation to the owner and asked to use their phone. With permission granted, he called Aspen Ward to provide us with the grim update.

After delivering the necessary information, Jason realised there was nothing more he could do at the scene, so he returned to his car and made his way back to the hospital.

As he approached St. Luke's, the sound of ambulance sirens pierced the air, shattering the otherwise tranquil surroundings.

An hour later, the police confirmed the identity of the deceased.

It was Brian.

The tragic circumstances became clearer: Brian had jumped in front of the 12:25 p.m. non-stop fast train and was declared dead at the scene.

The confirmation of Brian's identity and the calculated nature of his actions revealed that he had meticulously planned his suicide. He had taken great care to ensure his final act would be successful, adhering to his care plan until the very end, leaving no room for error this time.

Apparently, Brian had sat by the side of the tracks, smoking a cigar in the minutes before the train approached. I couldn't begin to imagine what was going through his mind at the time, but it was clear that he was resolute in following through with his plan. He left no note, spoke to no one about his intent.

His sister was devastated.

The news of Brian's death evoked intense emotions of shock, disbelief, grief, guilt, and sadness within the staff team. Those of us who believed we had developed a rapport with him struggled the most. The psychiatrist involved in his care was particularly shocked and felt let down. I think we all felt stressed, and our anxiety about our ability to prevent future incidents grew. Our confidence took a massive hit, and we began to question our capacity to provide effective care.

We all wondered whether we could have done more to prevent his suicide. Did we miss any warning signs? Could we have done more? Our belief in our ability to support and safeguard patients was deeply shaken.

Brian's suicide also had a significant impact on the therapeutic environment of the ward, affecting his fellow patients in various ways. Their emotions ranged from anger and sadness to confusion and frustration. Some patients directed their anger towards Brian, feeling betrayed by his actions. Others expressed sadness for him, recognising the pain he must have been experiencing. A few patients directed their anger toward us, questioning why we hadn't done more to prevent the tragedy. This dynamic created tension on the ward, disrupting the sense of safety and trust that is so essential for therapeutic progress.

Ideally, the ward team should have openly addressed their emotions together, provided each other with mutual support, and worked to reassure patients while restoring a sense of stability and trust. However, this was easier said than done. As a bank nurse, I wasn't included in any of the ongoing discussions and meetings after the incident. It was one of the downsides of not being a permanent member of staff. At times, I felt very isolated. I was glad to have Mum and friends from S Group to offload too.

Brian's meticulous planning and the careful execution of his suicide plan showed a profound sense of despair and determination to follow through with his decision to end his life. Looking back, it seemed almost inevitable.

His actions revealed that, despite outward appearances, he had reached a point where he believed suicide was the only solution to his suffering.

In the aftermath of his suicide, the ward team engaged in discussions, critical reflection, and a review of their practices and procedures. While no direct blame was placed on the staff or the hospital, the review process yielded valuable insights into how suicide prevention protocols, staff training, and support systems could be improved. (*12)

Brian's suicide affected me deeply.

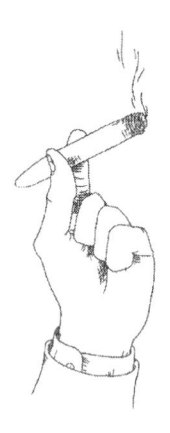

My Diary

A man on the ward took his own life yesterday. I had a nightmare about it last night. It was awful. Christ almighty!!! What a nightmare! I feel shocked and hurt, angry and sad about it all. None of us saw it coming and we can't figure out why. He had so much to live for and loads to look forward to. What a pain in the arse. They told us that he walked into the village and just sat by the side of the tracks, having a cigar, and waiting for the fast train to come before throwing himself in front of it. Just sat there!! Waiting!! Bugger me!!! Imagine that. I'd talked to him that morning about the plans to go and live near his sister and he seemed upbeat and happy – all the while knowing what he was going to do. FFS!!! What about the poor train driver? What a shocker. And the poor buggers from the police and the ambulance having to clear it all up. Christ all sodding mighty. He lied to me. To all of us! We were tricked by him. And I keep wondering if I missed anything. Did I? Did I???? Surely, I should have seen this coming? Surely ONE of us should have twigged what he was planning? NONE of us did. None. I keep running through the morning in my mind. Over and over and over again. The job we do is a hard one. We are not bloody mind readers!!!! We can't take the blame for someone choosing to end their own life. He did it to himself. Surely? And yet…. I feel so guilty and ashamed. Guilty that I did not see it coming. Ashamed that a life has ended. Fricking ashamed. I feel shit about myself. Absolute shit. None of us saw it coming. Not one of us. I keep crying. I'm okay for a bit and then I just burst into tears. I feel useless. When someone has a secret like that, there is nothing *you can do to make them share it. Christ, he was a bloody good actor! He fooled us all! Not one of us had the slightest inkling that he would do that. He was so angry about his wife leaving him. He said he would never get over it and he didn't. Poor bloke. Poor sad bloke. I wonder how she feels now? Poor woman, having to live with that for the rest of her life. Bugger. I'm struggling to make sense of it myself. I can't imagine how I would feel if it was Joe. I'd be so bloody furious with him. I'd never ever forgive him. It's not like you can ever ask him what the hell was he thinking? He played a blinder right to the end. At least he's out of it now. He must have been in agony. I hope wherever he's gone, he's at peace. For his sake, I really really do. Poor bloke.*

RIP Brian.

12
JAMES (JIMMY) MURPHY

"Where id was, there ego shall be."
The Ego and the Id (1923), Sigmund Freud

Our nurse manager, James (Jimmy) Murphy, exuded an aura of professionalism with his immaculate attire. Always dressed in a smart navy suit, crisp white shirt and designer tie, paired with shiny shoes, he presented himself well. Clean-shaven, with impeccably styled hair, and fingernails kept short and tidy, he had meticulous grooming.

The scent of his expensive aftershave preceded his arrival, earning him the playful jests of nurses who claimed you could smell Jimmy before seeing him. His distinct aroma lingered wherever he went and left an indelible mark on those around him. Jimmy's attention to detail in his appearance made him a memorable figure in the workplace.

Every hospital has its own version of Jimmy.

Despite not being particularly sharp or putting in too much effort, he managed to get by due to his sociable nature and infectious smile. With twinkling eyes and the luck and charm of the Irish, Jimmy seemed to navigate through challenges with ease. His ability to engage with others and bring a sense of joviality and 'Irish craic' endeared him to his colleagues and helped him skirt any potential consequences for his lack of diligence. Jimmy's affable personality and spirit made him a character beloved by many despite his many shortcomings in the workplace.

Jimmy had been promoted to a position far beyond his clinical ability, yet somehow managed to evade scrutiny. His likability was undeniable. With the 'gift of the gab,' he effortlessly recalled everyone's name and entertained others with humorous anecdotes and a willingness to engage in gossip. His warm demeanor ensured he always had time for a friendly chat.

Armed with his clipboard and writing pad, Jimmy exuded an air of bustling importance and authority as he traversed the corridors, smiling and conversing with everyone he met. Despite his elevated position, Jimmy's approachability and charm remained consistent, endearing him to colleagues at all levels and fostering a sense of teamwork throughout the hospital.

He was a well-known womaniser with a penchant for flirting and engaging in extramarital affairs, despite the knowledge of his long-suffering wife, Rosie. She was aware of his behaviour but didn't confront him or cause a scene in public. Instead, she chose to adopt a stance of silent endurance, choosing to ignore his indiscretions and continue with her life.

I wondered if her silent resignation suggested that she may have accepted Jimmy's behavior as part of their relationship dynamic, possibly influenced by her Catholic beliefs regarding the sanctity of marriage and the commitment to its permanence. Catholicism teaches that marriage is a sacrament, to be regarded as a lifelong commitment, regardless of the challenges and difficulties that may arise, and perhaps Rosie took this seriously. My mum was friendly with Rosie and admired her ability to put up with Jimmy and his nonsense.

Despite experiencing personal hurt and discomfort, Rosie seemed compelled to endure the situation—perhaps in the hope of upholding the sacredness of the marriage and keeping their family together. She was a classic Dublin beauty, with fair skin and red hair, while Jimmy carried the rugged charm of an Irish rogue. Despite their differences, they created the illusion of a loving couple in public, their affectionate gestures masking any underlying discord. Their ten-year-old son was the center of their world, a symbol of their shared love and devotion. They were a handsome little family.

Jimmy's latest squeeze was Mandy, a newly qualified staff nurse who had just made the move to St. Luke's from a training hospital up North. Her initial plan was to live in the nurse's residence to acquaint herself with the hospital and the local surroundings, with thoughts of potentially seeking out a house share down the line. Jimmy noticed her and targeted her at once. Fresh meat. Innocent. New. Just his style.

Staff noticed and started gossiping when they saw his unannounced visits to her ward, whisking her away to secluded areas like the office or the canteen for private conversations. It didn't take long for him to seduce her. As always with his conquests, Jimmy showed no discretion about their relationship, and they openly displayed affection with little regard for professional decorum.

While their brazen behavior blurred the lines between personal and professional boundaries, for some unknown reason, it didn't appear to undermine his position in the hospital. Any blame or judgment about the affair was inevitably heaped on the female participant's door.

Mandy was new to the hospital. She was lonely and naïve, unaware that she was just one of Jimmy's many romantic pursuits. Among the seasoned staff at the hospital, particularly the men of the Portering team, her involvement with Jimmy elicited a mix of disdain and begrudging admiration.

They recognised the familiar pattern, having seen Jimmy's affairs play out numerous times before. Their collective reaction was born from the repetitive nature of his workplace indiscretions and what could be described as institutional behaviour or an acceptance of behaviours that would not be considered acceptable outside of such a setting. They'd seen it all before.

Jimmy managed to evade consequences because he exuded such an amiable demeanor. He approached each day like a child in a candy store, encountering fresh opportunities for daily frolics and flirtation. Tales of his romantic escapades had become entrenched in St Luke's folklore. It was nearly impossible not to warm to him; he embodied the archetype of a mischievous yet endearing rogue.

There seemed to be a tacit acceptance that Jimmy's behaviour was simply part of who he was. His actions were excused under the guise of 'that's just Jimmy being Jimmy.'

Unlike the judgments and criticisms that would be leveled at others for similar infidelities, Jimmy seemed to operate under different rules. Somehow, he managed to escape the consequences and got away with it because he could. He always had.

Mandy confided in one of the nurses on her ward that Jimmy was her first love, and that from the moment they met, she knew he was special. Lovestruck, she believed in him, his shallow words wrapping her in a false but seductive blanket of affection. Mandy cherished every stolen glance and every whispered promise. In Jimmy's arms, she found solace, and in his eyes, she saw her future. He was her one and only.

Unsurprisingly, the nurse didn't keep her promise, and this juicy gossip spread like wildfire around St. Luke's.

Despite knowing Jimmy was married to Rosie, Mandy held onto the hope that one day he would choose her, envisioning a life where they'd walk hand in hand, where their love would blossom. Days turned into weeks, and weeks into months, but Jimmy remained tethered to Rosie, bound by obligations Mandy couldn't comprehend. She clung to the belief that their love would conquer all, that one day he would break free, and they would embrace their future together.

As time marched on, reality cast its shadow over Mandy's dreams. She watched helplessly as Jimmy's promises faded like echoes in the wind, swallowed by the harsh truth of his unyielding loyalty to Rosie. After yet another disappointing cancellation of their plans by Jimmy, she made up her mind to confront Rosie, tell her everything, and hold nothing back.

She was furious.

With the knowledge that Jimmy was on a late shift, Mandy seized the opportunity to visit Rosie at home.

As she sat in her car outside the house for a while, mustering the courage and gathering her thoughts before she spoke to Rosie, she was spotted by Eileen, Rosie's next-door neighbour. She'd heard the gossip and could hardly contain her excitement as she watched Mandy approach Rosie's doorstep in the quietness of the evening. Eileen's heart pounded with anticipation as she watched Mandy knock on the front door. She eased her lounge window open and stood behind the net curtain, straining to hear all she could.

Mandy's heart raced as she stood before Rosie, her palms clammy with nervous anticipation. The weight of her confession hung heavy in the air, threatening to suffocate her with each passing moment. She knew the truth would unleash a storm of emotions, shattering the fragile facade of their shared reality. In her dreams, Rosie would throw Jimmy out, and he would come to her to start their new and wonderful life together.

With trembling lips, Mandy began to speak, her words a delicate dance between honesty and regret. She told Rosie about the affair, how long it had been going on, where they had met, and of Jimmy's promises to her. Tears welled in her eyes as she recounted the moments she had shared with Jimmy.

Eileen could hardly breathe as she watched and listened.

Rosie remained silent throughout Mandy's revelation. Her eyebrows raised, eyes wide, fixed on Mandy's face. Her own face was blank. In the silence that followed the confession, Mandy braced herself for Rosie's wrath, her heart heavy with the burden of her story. But to her surprise, Rosie's gaze softened, she tutted and shook her head at her pityingly. When she finally spoke, the sharpness in Rosie's voice cut through the air like a knife, her words heavy with the weight of bitter truth as she pointed her finger at Mandy. "I know all about you, you sad silly cow. I've known since the beginning. You think you're the first? Don't be ridiculous. You're just one of many. This is what Jimmy does. It's who he is. Did you think he'd leave me for you? Wake up. Grow up. Stay away from married men, you pathetic bitch. Now fuck off and don't come here again."

Mandy's heart sank as she listened, the sting of Rosie's knowledge and accusations pierced the fragile veil of her illusions. Mandy felt the weight of Rosie's disappointment and anger bearing down upon her, the echoes of her own folly reverberating in those hissed words. In that moment, Mandy saw herself reflected in Rosie's eyes, a pitiful and foolish woman who had knowingly committed the sin of interfering with another woman's husband. He had no intention of leaving Rosie. Not now. Not ever.

Eileen stood rigid behind the curtain, heart banging, afraid to blink in case she missed something. She was absolutely itching to tell someone...

"I'm so sorry, Rosie," Mandy whispered, her gaze fixed on the doorstep.

She wished the ground would open and swallow her whole. She had never understood this saying before, but now, in her deep shame, its meaning was painfully clear.

Rosie stood firm on her doorstep, arms folded, her head shaking from side to side in disappointment as Mandy turned and walked away.

"You're not the first, and you certainly won't be the last," she mocked, her voice full of bitterness. "You fucking little bitch. I hope I never see your face again."

With those final words hanging heavy in the air, Rosie stared at Mandy as she walked to her car and watched, glaring as she drove away. Stepping back inside, closing the front door behind her, she leaned back on it with a mixture of anger and relief. "You fucking little shit, Jimmy. You fucking, sodding little shit," she whispered under her breath with gritted teeth.

Rosie knew that her neighbour had watched the whole debacle and that the gossip vultures were circling. Eileen wasted no time in picking up the phone. "Hey. You'll never guess what I've just seen..."

The hospital grapevine buzzed with excitement that night, the story embellished after each retelling, like Chinese whispers.

Mandy sped back to the nurses' home, grateful not to see anyone. She ran inside, up the stairs, and into her room. She locked the door behind her, flung herself on the bed, and wept. She'd immersed herself so deeply in Jimmy that she'd not made any new friends and realised she had no one to open her heart to at St. Luke's. She sobbed, wringing her hands in distress and shame, kicking herself for her stupidity. At 10 o'clock, she called in sick for the early shift the next day, feigning headache and flu symptoms. The weight of humiliation bore down heavily upon her, and she couldn't bear to face anyone. The thought of encountering anyone from St. Luke's filled her with dread. Berating herself mercilessly, and feeling like an utter fool, an absolute idiot, she retreated to bed. Curled up in the fetal position, cheeks flushed with embarrassment, heart pounding in her chest, she drifted into a fitful sleep for a few fragmented hours.

In the early hours of the morning, Mandy packed her belongings into plastic carrier bags and black sacks, listening and waiting until the sounds of people leaving for the early shift had ceased. Clothing, handbags, underwear, hairdryer, jewelry box, radio/cassette player, books and magazines, shoes and boots, perfume, toiletries, bedding and towels. It took less than an hour.

With her head hung low, she scurried down the stairs and hallway corridor, out of the side door and back a few times to fill her car with her bagged possessions, eager to leave without drawing any attention to herself. When her room was clear, she sat in the car and cried again. Taking a deep breath, she started the engine and drove slowly away from the building.

Stopping at the main entrance of the hospital, looking up at the nursing office, she saw that Matron Bain was on duty. Surveying her own tear-streaked, fatigued face in the rearview mirror, Mandy drew in another deep, unsteady breath. Gathering her resolve, she walked across the car park, through the front door, and quickly down the corridor, hunched forward, hugging its edge, her gaze fixed downward.

Finally, she reached the office door and tapped lightly. Matron, catching sight of Mandy's pale face, felt a surge of concern. Instantly, she recognised that something grave was unfolding. She rose from her seat, gently ushered Mandy into the office, and closed the door behind them, ensuring privacy. With a swift motion, she slid the sign on the door to "Engaged," signifying their need for uninterrupted conversation.

Mandy told her that she was leaving immediately, revealing that she had called in sick but couldn't foresee returning to her duties at St. Luke's.

With a somber tone, she disclosed the existence of pressing family matters that required her urgent presence up north. She said that she was sorry to leave like this, but she really had no choice. She slid her name badge and pass key across the desk toward Matron Bain as she spoke.

Matron had, of course, already heard on the grapevine that Mandy had visited Rosie and that she had then called in sick. To some degree, she had seen this coming but was surprised it was so soon. She pulled a chair closer to

Mandy and sat down beside her, her arm resting gently across Mandy's shoulders.

"Are you sure you want to do this? Think of your career. I've heard you have the makings of a fine nurse. Don't end your time with us like this. Whatever has happened will blow over, I'm sure."

"I've made a fool of myself. I've done something unforgivable. I need to go home."

This was said with such finality and resolve that Matron Bain's experience told her it was hopeless to try to talk her out of her decision. Quietly, she made them both a cup of tea and found some biscuits. Between sips, she elaborated on the standard protocol regarding notice periods, emphasising that exceptions could be made under extraordinary circumstances, subject to a recommendation from a nursing officer. As she observed the young woman seated beside her, her heart went out to her, witnessing the mixture of relief and anguish on her face.

With empathy, she agreed to facilitate the process for her.

Silent tears streamed down Mandy's cheeks as Matron efficiently completed the necessary paperwork, guiding her through the forms with kindness. With a gentle hand, showing Mandy where to sign, she offered quiet reassurance along the way. Amidst the paperwork, Matron Bain assured Mandy that she would handle the processing of the documents, promised to reach out to human resources, the ward manager, and the nurse's home on her behalf.

Then Matron asked practical and supportive questions: How long would the journey take? Did she know the route? Did she have enough petrol? Did she have money? Food and drink for the journey?

During her vulnerability, Matron's words provided Mandy with hope and support in such uncertainty. She encouraged Mandy to use the office telephone to call ahead and let her mother know she was making the journey home. Matron hadn't been fooled into believing the story about a family emergency, and this fact passed in silent acknowledgment between them. Refusing to listen to Mandy's protest to leave alone, Matron waited until Mandy was calm and safe to drive. Then she walked with her to her car, with a supportive hand on her arm. At the car, with a smile, she gave her a warm, motherly hug.

"Right now, drive safe, take care, and let me know you've arrived. This isn't the end of the world. You've your whole life ahead of you. Concentrate on your career. You'll find better than Jimmy Murphy, you can be sure of that!"

Mandy thanked her, waving sheepishly as she drove away with a wry smile and a quivering lip.

Returning to the office, a whirlwind of emotions accompanied Matron Bain. The shrill ringing telephone greeted her as she opened the door, its urgency a reminder of the perpetual flow of challenges in the hospital. "Hello, Matron Bain. How can I help you?" she answered, then proceeded to deal with the next problem. Like the time and the tide, hospital life continued regardless.

When Jimmy arrived to take over for the late shift, Matron was ready for him. After giving him a professional handover, she fixed him with a stern stare.

Jimmy returned her gaze innocently, unaware that Mandy had left the hospital.

"What's wrong?" he asked. "Is everything alright?"

"James Murphy, I'll say this once and only once," Matron Bain began firmly. "Your philandering and canoodling will get you into big trouble one day. How or why Rosie puts up with you, I'll never know."

Jimmy started to retort, but she raised her hand to silence him. "I am speaking, James Murphy. And you will listen." She glared at him.

Jimmy's expression shifted, realising she meant business. He sat waiting for her to continue, understanding the gravity of her admonition but not yet what it was about.

"Your latest conquest left today," Matron continued, her voice tinged with disappointment. "Mortified and broken-hearted with what you put her through. It can't keep happening, Jimmy. It must stop."

"I don't know what you're talking about, Matron. Conquest? What? When? Who?" Jimmy stammered, his confusion evident in his voice and face.

"You know perfectly well. Don't play your games with me. You really think you're something special, don't you? Well, let me tell you. Mandy. Mandy Cooper. Staff Nurse Mandy Cooper. You know the one? The same Mandy you've been fooling with these last six months."

"She's gone?" exclaimed Jimmy, clearly shocked at the news.

Matron Bain nodded gravely. "Yes, she's gone. And it's no surprise. Your behaviour has consequences, and it's time you faced them."

Jimmy's expression had shifted from innocence to a mixture of disbelief and regret. He hadn't anticipated this outcome, despite his actions. "I didn't mean for her to leave. I do care about her," he said, his voice tinged with remorse.

Matron Bain sighed heavily.

"Really? Caring isn't enough, Jimmy. Your actions speak louder than words. You need to understand the impact of your behaviour on your wife and son, and those around you, especially your colleagues. This hospital has lost a skilled staff nurse because of you. No one else. You're a bloody disgrace. You dirty dog."

Jimmy hung his head, shamed by the weight of her direct words. He couldn't undo what had been done, but he also recognised the need to change his ways.

"I'm sorry," Jimmy said, his voice barely above a whisper. "I'll do better. I'll make things right."

The dust settled.

People soon forgot about Mandy. Jimmy repented. He made things right with Rosie and, for a while, became a model husband and father. He tried hard to reign himself in. Then, one day, ten months later, while visiting a ward, he spotted a new nursing assistant. Young, attractive, and eager to please, she introduced herself as Sandra.

"Well now Sandra, tell me what your plans are for the future," beamed Jimmy as she gazed up at him in awe, wide-eyed like a rabbit dazzled in car headlights.

"Is your plan to do your nurse training here at St. Luke's? If so, perhaps that's something I can help you with..."

The cycle of temptation and indulgence repeated itself, despite his previous promises and efforts to change.

James Murphy was off again.

My Diary

Apparently old Jimbo Murphy has been at it again. Mandy. She was such a quiet soul. Came all the way here to work and Jimmy got his claws into her. Now she's legged it. I don't blame her. Fancy her going round to see Rosie! Eileen was quick off the mark telling everyone. It went round like wildfire. What a show-up. I don't know what they all see in him. Too smarmy for my liking. Always smells nice, though. He must spend a fortune on aftershave. None of your Old Spice for Jimbo. How does he get away with it? His poor wife, what she's had to put up with over the years.

Poor Joe—one sniff at someone else, and I made sure he was out the door! I would never have taken him back. I sort of admire women who can. But not me. One strike and you're out. I don't think I'll ever get married again. What's the point? It would take someone special... IS there such a man? Not a man like Jimmy anyway. What a nightmare.

13
MY DIARY

"Preserve your memories, keep them well, what you forget you can never retell."
Louisa May Alcott

I've always kept a diary. I'm quite a private person and I'm not someone who finds it easy to talk about my feelings. I've found that it's a good way for me to express myself. It helps to create order in my mind, and it's a way to process it all when things feel chaotic. It's like having a silent ear to pour my heart out to. No judgment or negativity. When I look back on some of the stuff I've written, I could cringe sometimes. But it's a great reminder of what was happening and how I felt about things at the time. I never show my diary to anyone. I don't talk about it. I don't know if Joe ever read it—he never said if he did. I hope he didn't. I don't write in it every day. I haven't committed to maintaining it daily—it's too time-consuming. I'm too busy for that. I just write more when I'm upset, angry, or mega happy. Lots of good and bad stuff in *My Diary*. It's been so valuable since I started nurse training. It's my only way of reflecting and getting stuff out of my head, putting it onto paper. There isn't always the support for us in the "caring" professions... we learn to get on with it all, keep on going, not complain. Be more stoic. It's a case of "physician heal thyself."

Anne Frank was given a diary on her 13th birthday in 1942. At first, she used it to record her observations about friends and school and her own thoughts, but when her family went into hiding, it became a war document. She rewrote it when the Dutch government asked people to document the Nazi occupation. I know she described herself as "a bundle of contradictions." This rings true for me too. On the outside, as a nurse, you must appear to be in control, no matter what happens and despite how you feel on the inside. There've been times when I've felt really scared, sick, and like running away. But you've got to face it all. It's an act, really. An observer would have no idea how freaked out, incompetent, and afraid

I've felt. I've seen and heard about some awful, gruesome stuff, even in my short career so far.

Now and again, I flick through my old diaries, remembering people and times past. I found this next entry from my third-year student days that made me laugh out loud. Casting my mind back, I remembered the incident on Juniper Ward vividly.

My Diary

Bloody Graham! I feel really stupid. And ANGRY. How the hell was I to know she would smuggle alcohol into the ward in her toiletries? Sneaky or what!!?? She acted like butter wouldn't melt in her mouth. I wondered why she kept going to the toilet... I'm not sure addictions are for me. I don't really get it. I don't know why someone would come in for a detox, saying they wanted help, and then do that. Graham was well out of order having a pop at me.

I'm in my third year though—perhaps I'm not cut out for all this. I should have known better. I don't want to go in tomorrow. I could call in sick. I feel sick thinking about it! What a shitshow. I can't do that. I'll have to get past it. I'll force myself to go in. What a bummer...

14
RUBY

"All the suffering, stress, and addiction comes from not realising you already are what you are looking for."
Jon Kabat-Zinn

Juniper Ward. Early shift.
Drug and Alcohol Assessment and Detox Unit. Mixed sex. 30 beds.

The drug and alcohol unit at St Luke's was named Juniper Ward, which I always found ironic. It was designed to provide specialised care for individuals struggling with substance use disorders and offered a range of treatment options to support recovery. Juniper was a clinical placement in my third year of training, and by then, we were often expected to take charge of the ward with minimal supervision.

The importance of addressing substance use disorders within psychiatric settings and providing comprehensive and holistic care to individuals struggling with addiction, was becoming increasingly recognised. The unit played a crucial role in helping patients achieve and maintain recovery from drug and alcohol dependence.

Upon admission, patients underwent a thorough assessment to gauge the extent of their substance use disorder and identify any accompanying mental health issues. For those facing withdrawal symptoms, the ward offered medical detoxification to ensure a safe and managed process. Care plans typically included a combination of medical, psychological, and social interventions.

My first assignment for the day was to admit and assess Ruby, a middle-aged woman seeking a planned alcohol detox for the second time. She arrived promptly at 9 a.m. as arranged. A polished professional HR manager in a multinational corporation, Ruby exuded sophistication with her impeccable grooming, designer attire and handbag, and flawless makeup.

Beneath her outward success lay a dependence on alcohol that was intertwined with her career demands.

Business engagements, boozy lunches, and client entertainment were integral to her role, all of which typically involved alcohol consumption.

Ruby had been advised to stop drinking for twelve hours before admission. The symptoms of alcohol withdrawal generally begin within twelve to forty-eight hours and include nausea, headaches, vomiting, and sleep problems. Without intervention, the withdrawal symptoms can worsen significantly. Alcohol withdrawal poses a significant risk due to its combined psychological and physical impacts. Thankfully, medical advancements have led to the development of various medications and therapies aimed at mitigating these symptoms.

Ruby's detox plan spanned fourteen days, during which she would receive a standard reducing regime of Librium. This medication has calming and sedative properties, specifically targeting anxiety symptoms. By easing the initial surge of alcohol withdrawal—often considered one of the most challenging phases—Librium was prescribed to facilitate a smoother transition for Ruby during her detoxification process.

The admission process seemed to go well. Despite saying she felt slightly sick and shaky, Ruby was articulate, engaged, and appeared motivated. I felt a real connection with her, and I enjoyed taking her history and hearing about her life. By 10:30 a.m., I'd completed the paperwork, taken an inventory of Ruby's property, introduced her to the other patients, shown her around the ward, and pointed out her bed in the dormitory.

At 11 o'clock, it was coffee time, which both staff and patients usually shared in the ward lounge. Ruby had already received her first dose of Librium and told me she was starting to feel less shaky and more settled.

At midday, lunch was served, and she ate a modest portion before joining the other patients in the lounge area.

I was chatting to Graham, the ward manager, in the corridor when Ruby passed us on her way to the lounge. She gave me a friendly wink, a thumbs up, and a warm smile. I was pleased to sense a growing connection forming between us and anticipated a budding therapeutic rapport that held promise.

Feeling pretty chuffed with myself and my nursing skills, I smiled back at her. I was taken aback to see Graham's eyes widen. "Office. Now," he demanded.

"What did you notice as Ruby passed us, Claire?" Graham probed as soon as the door closed. He looked angry, his face red and tense.

"Nothing. Why? Did I miss something?"

"Alcohol? The smell of al...co...hol?"

"No, I didn't. Are you sure?"

Graham's eyes narrowed. "Go and sit in the lounge with the patients. See what you notice and report back. Did you complete her property inventory?"

"Okay. Yes. Yes, I did. Is something wrong?"

"Do as I've asked and do it now," Graham hissed sternly.

I felt confused, wondering what he was talking about. But, as requested, I sat in the lounge for the next hour, carefully observing the patients and my surroundings, feeling a bit narked. I detected nothing out of the ordinary, nor did I catch any scent of alcohol lingering in the air. I had no idea what Graham was going on about.

Meanwhile, Ruby made a couple of trips to the ladies' room, returning each time to her seat, chatting with the other patients and watching the television. I watched her routine and saw how she carefully placed her designer handbag on the floor beside her chair.

As Ruby returned from her third trip to the restroom, I couldn't help but notice a slight unsteadiness in her gait and the drooping of her eyes. "Are you feeling okay, Ruby?"

With a slightly slurred response, she replied, "Yesh, I'm fine, thanksh."

It was then that I detected a faint but unmistakable aroma of alcohol. My concern deepened, and I legged it to the nursing office, where I found Graham waiting for me.

He looked up expectantly as I entered. "Well?" he inquired.

"I think you're right. I can smell alcohol. But how?"

Graham's response was firm and direct. "Did you check her belongings? Really check? Did you open every bottle, check in every compartment?" he questioned.

I shook my head.

"Well, no," I confessed. "I didn't realise I had to do that."

"This is a drug and alcohol unit," Graham emphasised. "We trust no one. We are alert. We are suspicious. We have eyes in the back of our heads. We are awake! We are on our toes! We must always be vigilant. Come with me. Now."

Graham proceeded to the lounge. His tone firm yet composed, he led Ruby quietly to the privacy of her designated bed area, with me trailing meekly behind, feeling a sense of unease. Once there, Graham addressed Ruby directly, his concern evident in his voice. "Ruby, we suspect that you have been drinking," he stated bluntly.

With sleepy eyes, Ruby adamantly shook her head. "No, Graham, shertainly not," she replied, her words slurred.

He asked Ruby for permission to inspect her handbag.

"Shertainly, you may," Ruby responded, taking an unsteady step backward as she opened the clasp, allowing him to peer inside. Her designer handbag contained no trace of alcohol.

Graham then told me to get another staff member to help and thoroughly examine all the bathrooms. Our search yielded a collection of Ruby's designer toiletries: shampoo, conditioner, body lotions, shower gels, creams, and ointments on the windowsill and vanity unit. There was no obvious evidence of alcohol.

Drawing on his years of experience, Graham instructed us to check each bottle, his voice firm and decisive. So, with meticulous attention, we examined each container. To my dismay, nine out of the ten bottles were filled not with toiletries, but with alcohol. It was evident that Ruby had been sneaking away to the toilets to indulge herself. The revelation left me stunned as I realised the extent of Ruby's deception. I felt stupid.

I'd learnt that alcoholism can manifest in various ways and that individuals often lie and deceive as they attempt to conceal their addiction or justify their behaviour.

Many alcoholics struggle with denial about the severity of their addiction and feel ashamed or embarrassed. Lying allows them to maintain a façade of normality and avoid confronting the reality of their situation. Lying and cheating are often symptoms of the underlying addiction and should be addressed with compassion and support. Encouraging honesty and providing opportunities for treatment can help individuals struggling with alcoholism confront their addiction and begin the journey to recovery.

Graham was compassionate with Ruby but not with me.

"You're a third-year student nurse, Claire. You should have known better. I'm not impressed," he snapped.

"I apologise, Graham, and I hold my hands up. Not for a minute did I think Ruby would smuggle drink into the ward. She seemed so committed to having the detox, I just didn't expect it."

"That's the nature of addiction," Graham said, barely acknowledging my apology. "You must be on it from now on for their sake as well as your own. It's not good enough. You're a third year. Not a first year."

"I agree. I'm sorry, Graham," I mumbled, recognising the serious implications of the situation moving forward.

Embarrassment burned as I realised my rookie mistake, and I knew it would be discussed in handover. I feared the judgement of my colleagues and hoped my mistake wouldn't cause Graham to fail me on this placement, jeopardising the completion of my training. Understanding that Ruby's addiction drove her deception didn't ease my frustration. I'd put time and energy into nurturing our therapeutic bond, and she'd chucked it back in my face. Graham's telling off added to my humiliation, igniting anger toward both him and Ruby, but most of all toward myself.

I was desperate for the shift to end, desperate to flee the disgrace.

At the end of the shift, Graham spoke with me privately. I think he knew how upset I was.

"Don't take it too personally," he began. "I have to be tough on you because of the challenges in this placement. Hopefully, it'll be a learning experience for you."

"Okay. Thanks."

Tears of shame burned as I walked to my car that evening. I felt so foolish and embarrassed. I could hardly sleep, tossing and turning, going over it and asking myself why I'd got it so wrong.

The following day, I was reluctant to return to Juniper Ward and, for the first time during my training, considered phoning in sick to avoid the embarrassment.

Instead, I pushed myself to go in for the late shift, still feeling ashamed. To my surprise, there was no mention of my mistake. It seemed to have been forgotten already. On my break, I asked one of the staff nurses for advice.

"Don't dwell on it; it's another day. We've got plenty else to do," he replied, lightening the mood. "Nobody's dead, are they? We all cock up sometime. You're going to experience much worse in this game. You cocked up. Nobody's dead. Get over yourself and just keep going!"

15
ADA

"Being a nurse is weird: I can keep a poker face through trauma but have a mental breakdown over losing my favourite pen".
Unknown

Cedar Ward. Early shift.
Psychogeriatric Ward. Mixed sex. 30 beds.

Ruth, the nurse in charge of Cedar Ward, may have been petite in stature, but her presence was anything but small. Quick and nimble, she moved about the ward with effortless grace, her every step purposeful and efficient. Despite her diminutive frame, she possessed boundless energy and a tireless work ethic that set her apart. She tackled her responsibilities head-on, never hesitating to lend a helping hand or meet a challenge. Her dedication was unwavering, and she approached each task with meticulous attention to detail.

She had a knack for anticipating the needs of her patients and her team, ensuring that everything ran smoothly. Her colleagues knew they could always rely on her to get the job done. Ruth was a steadfast anchor, guiding Cedar Ward with her quick wit, sharp mind, and compassionate heart.

One Sunday morning, I was acting as 'runner' while Ruth dispensed the patients' medications. Her attention to detail extended to the precise administration of each patient's medication. Armed with their individual drug charts, she methodically dispensed the prescribed drugs into small plastic containers, ensuring accuracy. With each container carefully labelled, Ruth would relay the patient's name to me. I, in turn, would repeat the name back to confirm accuracy. Only when we both agreed would I take the medication to the patient, verifying their identity with Ruth once more before administering the tablets.

Strictly 'by the book,' this system of double-checking ensured that every patient received the correct medication in the correct dosage, minimising the risk of errors and prioritising safety.

I loved working on Sunday mornings. Unlike the busy weekdays, Sundays unfolded at a more leisurely pace, devoid of the usual ward rounds and hectic routines. Instead, the atmosphere was calm and relaxed, offering a welcome respite from the week's demands. With fewer tasks demanding our immediate attention, we found precious time to connect with the patients on a deeper level, listening attentively to their stories and offering comfort and encouragement.

As the sun filtered through the windows of Cedar Ward, this Sunday morning began as usual with a comforting breakfast spread. The aroma of freshly cooked porridge mingled with the savoury scent of sizzling sausages, crispy bacon, scrambled eggs, and toast. The clinking of cutlery against plates and the hum of conversation filled the room as everyone enjoyed the relaxed breakfast.

I moved among the patients, personally delivering their prescribed medications as I double-checked with Ruth and ensured that everyone received their breakfast with care. A televised church service was shown in the lounge, providing spiritual nourishment for those unable to attend in person. Patients could also choose to attend the hospital chapel for a service, finding solace in communal worship.

I noticed Ada's unusual behaviour with concern. Ada, who was typically composed, appeared visibly agitated. She seemed unable to find her usual calm or settle for breakfast. I approached her gently, offering a reassuring hand on her shoulder.

"Ada, is everything alright?"

Ada paused, her expression clouded with confusion. "I... I'm not sure," she replied hesitantly, her voice trembling slightly. She pushed my hand away, glared at me, and walked quickly across the room. Then she stood very still, looking lost.

Ruth was watching from the drug trolley and gestured for me to keep an eye on her. As breakfast finished, the kitchen staff began their routine of clearing tables and tidying up. Plates were swiftly collected, cups gathered, and leftover food disposed of. A small pile of cooked sausages remained on a plate, keeping warm on the hot trolley nearby.

My heart sank as I saw Ada's mounting distress. "Ada, it's alright," I said softly, trying to calm her. "Let's sit down and have a chat. We'll make sure you get something to eat."

But Ada's agitation only escalated. Fixing her gaze on the sausages, her voice rose in frustration. "I haven't finished! I haven't had my breakfast!" she insisted, stamping her feet, her words filled with desperation. "Don't take it away! I'm hungry!"

She launched herself at the hot trolley, grabbing a sausage in each hand, her face terrified. I understood something was wrong and wanted to help, but her refusal to listen only heightened the tension.

"Ada, please, let's talk about this. I'm here to help you."

Before I could stop her, Ada frantically stuffed a whole sausage into her mouth. She thrust it in so quickly that it became lodged in her throat. Her face turned red, her eyes bulged, and tears streamed down her face as she struggled to breathe and tried to cough.

Ruth slammed the drug trolley shut and rushed over to help. I had already begun patting Ada's back, but her lips were turning blue.

Ruth acted quickly. She tried to reach the sausage with her finger, but it was lodged too far back. I was already behind Ada, ready to perform the Heimlich manoeuvre. Ruth stepped back as I began the rapid upward thrusts on Ada's abdomen. With each thrust, I felt the tension in her body, the desperate need for air.

Ruth, her heart racing, silently urged me on. After the third thrust, there was still no movement. In desperation, Ruth pushed me aside, and with unbelievable strength, grabbed Ada, lifted her up, turned her upside down, and shook her. With her legs in the air, the sausage shot out of her mouth, landing with a wet thud on the floor. Ruth carefully turned Ada back upright, sitting her gently on the floor.

Ada sat gasping for air, tears streaming down her face. Ruth was also gasping, sitting beside her, offering comfort while I knelt next to them, feeling shaky and nauseous. The incident had likely taken just minutes, but it felt like an eternity. My head was woozy, and I was sweating profusely.

The room was filled with the sound of Ada's ragged breathing and the collective sigh of relief from everyone watching. The other patients and staff had fallen silent.

After a few moments, Ada's breathing steadied, and her colour began to return. Ruth and I exchanged a glance, both silently acknowledging the gravity of the situation.

"Are you okay, Ada?" Ruth asked gently, placing a hand on her shoulder.

Ada nodded, still shaken. "I'm hungry. Where's my sausage?" she croaked, her voice hoarse from the choking.

We burst out laughing at her request. The tension that had filled the room just moments earlier melted away.

"Sausage?" Ruth repeated incredulously, laughter bubbling up uncontrollably. "You're having a laugh! It'll be porridge for you today, Ada!"

Ada joined in, despite her hoarseness. Smiling, we helped her to her feet and sat her at the table, where one of the staff was already placing a small bowl of porridge and a cup of tea. We left Ada in their care and headed to the nursing office.

As we closed the office door, we clung to each other, overcome with hysterical laughter.

"Crikey, Ruth, that was a close one! Where on earth did you find the strength to lift her up like that? I couldn't believe it!"

"I don't know," Ruth squeaked between giggles, wiping away tears of laughter. "I have absolutely no idea!"

During the handover to the late shift, I relished recounting the sausage-choking incident, infusing the story with dramatic effect. Ruth's quick thinking and heroic actions earned laughter and applause from the team.

"You're Superwoman, Ruth!" one of them exclaimed. The nickname stuck, and Ruth became known as 'Superwoman,' a title that made her feel both embarrassed and proud.

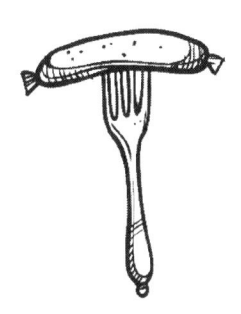

My Diary

Choking on a sausage. I'm never going to forget the look on Ruth's face and her spinning Ada around. That sausage shot out like it was fired from a gun. What a day! It could have turned out so bad. After it, I felt shaky. Even though I was laughing, I felt weird. It makes me realise that death is never far away. That was a really close one! I'll never look at a sausage again without thinking of Ada. Or Ruth. Superwoman.

16
THE STAFF MUGS

"You can't be everyone's cup of tea, otherwise you'd be a mug."
Unknown

I started noticing a practice that seemed peculiar to nurses during each clinical placement in my training, something that always amused and fascinated me. The mugs used by staff for coffee and tea breaks on the ward, and during staff handovers were often personalised or had humorous, customised designs. Each staff member owned their own mug, and under no circumstances was it to be used by anyone else.

Inexperienced staff or students who made the tea tray without knowing this would unwittingly commit a grave mistake by choosing random mugs from the staff cupboard. Their innocent efforts would be met with head shakes, tutting, eye rolls, and smirks from the rest of the team.

The mugs provided a sense of identity among the nursing team, adding humour and stress relief to our challenging work environment. Each mug had a story behind it. Some were printed with names, titles, or a favourite quote.

Staff would take their mugs with them when they moved to a different workplace. Yet, some mugs remained, forgotten at the back of the cupboard for years, waiting for their owners to reclaim them. These mugs were never thrown out—just in case the owner returned, or as a sentimental reminder of those who had left.

Nursing assistant Gladys Peacock had worked on the same ward for decades. She remembered the owner of every mug in the cupboard and loved to tell stories about them. She took care of the mugs, especially those abandoned long ago, pushing them to the back of the cupboard and stuffing them with paper towels.

A chunky blue mug that said, "Frankie Says Relax" had once belonged to a charge nurse named Frankie, who had left St Luke's to work in New Zealand. Gladys hoped he'd return one day and she made it her business to look after his mug until then.

A small bone china mug decorated with poppies had belonged to a doctor who had long since passed away.

The owner of a chubby green Canterbury pottery mug had been a staff nurse who gave up nursing and now worked in a bank.

The mugs, like their owners, came in all shapes, sizes, and colours. There were classic ceramic mugs, sturdy and reliable, as well as flimsy porcelain teacups, chunky mason jar mugs, solid pottery mugs, fun colour-changing mugs, utility enamel camping mugs, quirky animal-shaped mugs, huge tankard-sized mugs, and tiny dainty cups.

Gladys's own vintage mug was adorned with bold orange and brown geometric patterns characteristic of the 1970s. It had come from a set that had belonged to her mother. When Gladys went on holiday, she would take her mug home, carefully wrapped in paper towels. Before her days off, she would wash her mug meticulously, stuff it with paper towels to prevent insects from crawling inside—or worse, other staff from using it—and then push it to the back of the cupboard.

I, too, had my own mug that I kept in my work bag. It was a blue mug with a large gold "C" on the front. The few times I'd forgotten it and left it behind on a ward, someone always returned it to me.

Because it was **my** mug. "Claire's Mug."

17
SELINA

"Don't cry because it's over, smile because it happened."
Dr Seuss

Briar Ward. Early shift.
Psychogeriatric Ward. Female. 35 beds.

Selina was the nurse in charge for the early Sunday morning shift on Briar Ward. She was a large, jolly nurse from Jamaica who had come to England in the early seventies as one of the Windrush nurses. (*13) She told me that she was lucky to be employed in elderly care, and she was passionate about it.

Selina met and married a local carpenter within a year of arriving, and together they had three children. They lived in one of the hospital houses on Hospital Crescent, a cluster of three-bedroom semi-detached houses at the bottom of the long drive to the hospital.

She'd kept her broad Jamaican accent, endearing herself to all of us with her authenticity. She had a knack for speaking her mind, laughing heartily, offering gentle reprimands when necessary, and approaching both her profession and her Christian faith with utmost seriousness.

Selina often treated the ward team to the rich flavours of Jamaican cuisine. Her offerings included succulent jerk chicken, savoury ackee and saltfish, and the delightful bammy—a crispy yet fluffy flatbread made from ground cassava soaked in coconut milk and fried to perfection. Her culinary contributions not only satisfied appetites but also brought a taste of her culture and warmth to the hospital environment.

Her passion for cooking and nourishing others was undeniable, and her ample physique attested to her love for indulging in the delicious meals she prepared. When she laughed, it was a joyous spectacle; her whole body moved and jiggled in rhythm with her laughter, filling the room with warmth and contagious happiness and we couldn't help but join in. Her laughter reverberated throughout the ward, echoing down the corridors, and lifting spirits wherever it reached. It began with a subtle giggle, gradually building to a resounding crescendo of joy.

At its peak, Selina would remove her glasses, leaning forward as she slapped her hands on her thighs, consumed by laughter. Tears of mirth streamed down her face as she exclaimed, "Oh my, oh my, oh my! That's sooo funny! Lord help me! Oh Lord! What would people be tinkin'?" Her laughter was a testament to her vibrant spirit.

She'd asked for extra staff on the ward that morning. Two patients required end-of-life care, and I was more than happy to help. When I was a student, Selina had been my mentor during my care-of-the-elderly placement. I'd completed the death-and-dying module with her supervising and supporting me through my very first experience of death.

I'd been terrified about seeing death firsthand. I think I'd built it up to be something scary, something to be avoided at all costs. My fear of the unknown, my lack of knowledge about what to expect, and my vivid imagination had fuelled my fears. The way she supported me and the gentle way she spoke to patients as they were dying touched my heart. I admired her natural teaching ability, wisdom, and religious beliefs. She was full of warmth and had a deep respect for life and death. Her deep brown eyes shone with kindness, and compassion oozed from every part of her large body. Her teachings stayed with me.

At St. Luke's, if death was expected, every effort was made to ensure that the patient did not die alone. A family member or nurse was rostered to sit with them until the very end. The nursing staff did this gladly, especially for those who had no family to sit with them. Selina believed that it was an honour to be at the bedside of someone as they made their transition out of this world and that there was an incredible sacredness as they took their last breath.

Her belief was that each death should be special. It may sound strange, but she made the effort to make death special for every person, viewing it as a privilege. She ensured the atmosphere was quiet and supportive and the patient was as pain-free as possible. Having worked as an aide in hospice care in Jamaica, she brought her wealth of knowledge and skills to St. Luke's to share with the staff.

Her belief was that when death occurred, it was a time to take a deep breath, to stop, and be present with what was happening—sitting mindfully at the bedside. The aim of end-of-life care is to attend fully to the patient's needs and comfort, offering respectful, gentle care, easing them out of this world with dignity.

I took over from the nurse on the night shift. I'd been brought in with the sole task of alternating each hour between the two end-of-life patients, moving from one to the other and taking over from the previous nurses.

Doris was a tiny bird of a lady. Her thin skin stretched over her face, her lips sunken without her false teeth, and her eyes closed deep in fallen sockets. Nestled into the pillows, Doris lay on her right side with her left arm outside the covers, her skin almost translucent, a simple gold band hanging loosely on her wedding ring finger. Her breath was barely there—just the slightest movement of her chest and hardly a flicker behind her paper-thin eyelids. Death was not far away. I felt for her pulse. It was barely there, maybe fifteen beats a minute, if that.

The dormitory was quiet.

Briar Ward prided itself on good personal care. Patients were turned regularly—from side to back, to side again. Pressure areas on the buttocks, heels, shoulder blades, back of the head, backs of the knees, and elbows were proactively cared for. Mouth, eye, and ear care were given diligently. We spoke in whispers and walked quietly between the beds as the morning sun cast delicate shafts of light through the windows onto the yellow and beige striped curtains pulled between each bed. The radio played softly in the background.

Doris had just been turned and was peaceful. I sat quietly at her bedside and placed my hand over hers.

"Hi, Doris, it's Claire here. I don't know if you remember me, but I'm here to take care of you today and help keep you comfortable."

Selina's head popped through the curtains, and she grinned at me, her big white teeth and sparkling eyes beaming from her large brown face. She mouthed silently, "Okay?" I nodded, smiled back, and gave her the thumbs up.

She disappeared and returned a few minutes later with a cup of tea for me, placing it on the bedside table. She silently felt Doris's pulse, looked at me knowingly, and made a face that said, "Not long now." She nodded and whispered, "I will be back to help you turn."

I quietly prepared the bedside, moving the personal care trolley and adjusting the bed. Selina returned as promised. Working together, we began the process of turning Doris over to her left side and making her comfortable again.

Before we started, Selina gently touched Doris on the shoulder and bent to talk quietly to her. "Hello, Doris, my dear," she whispered. "We're just going to turn you over to your other side and make you more comfortable, dahlin'."

I tucked the slide sheet under Doris's right hip, and together we gently rolled her onto her back, then pulled the slide sheet through and rolled her over to her left side. She was so tiny that there was no need to use a hoist. She rolled over easily. Selina lifted her pale pink nightdress and gently checked her elbows, knees, sacrum, and hips for any signs of redness or broken skin. Everything was fine. The padded pants she wore for incontinence were dry. Selina glanced knowingly at me, her eyes filled with compassion.

We placed a slim pillow between her knees, straightened her nightdress, ensuring no folds or creases pressed into her skin.

We talked to her the whole time, murmuring words of reassurance. "There you are. Just popping a pillow between your knees, Doris. Just turning you over. There you go, that's better, isn't it? Soon be finished. Sorry to disturb you."

Satisfied that she was comfortable, Selina arranged the pillows and pulled up the sheet and duvet, tucking it in around her.

I was the first to notice something had changed and gestured silently to Selina. We both leaned forward to look closer. Doris had indeed exhaled her final breath. Her face had relaxed, her jaw slightly sagged. Her body was completely limp.

She was dead.

With an expected death like this, there is no drama. No need for crash trolleys, shouting, or panic. It's not an emergency. We both looked at our watches and made a mental note of the time.

Hearing is widely thought to be the last sense to go in the dying process, and Selina was mindful of this as she rested her hand on Doris's forehead. "Bless you, dahlin'," she whispered, and then asked me to open the window "to set her spirit free."

"We now have an opportunity to be quiet and present, so let's just take it and thank de Lord God Almighty," Selina said.

Absorbed by the enormity of the event, we stood quietly together for a few moments by the bed, witnessing the passing of Doris's life.

I reflected on the wisdom Selina had imparted when I was a student. Being present in the moments after death is an incredible thing. It can be a gift to the people you're with, and a gift to the person who's just died. They're starting their final journey. Keeping a calm space around their body, and in the room, means their journey starts in a peaceful way. Selina didn't just talk the talk. In her life and her clinical practice, she walked the walk.

Softly, we turned Doris onto her back, placing one pillow under her head, making sure her mouth did not gape open. We placed her hands gently across her tummy, with her legs and feet together, and her nightdress tucked in securely around her. Her eyes were closed.

I quickly popped into the clinic room to collect the "death box," tucked away in the corner. Lifting its lid carefully, I found everything needed for the final rites. Shrouds, disposable aprons, gloves, identification bands, mouth care equipment, bags for waste, scissors, gauze, towels, and clean sheets—each item held significance for the last offices. I methodically checked the inventory, ensuring everything was in place.

Returning to the bedside, I saw that Selina had already placed Doris's toiletries and hairbrush ready. A bowl of hot water and linen skip stood waiting.

Selina sent another nurse to help me and immediately began completing the necessary paperwork and procedures following a death. She started by telephoning the on-call doctor to certify the death and instructed the ward clerk to contact Doris's only next of kin, a distant cousin in Australia.

I drew the curtains firmly around the bed and began caring for Doris one last time.

My Diary

I've worked with some fantastic nurses. I've also worked with some awful ones. Mum said 'learn from the good ones – forget the bad ones' Good advice. I love working with Selina. It's a weird thing to say but even a death with her is a good thing. I remember the first dead person I saw was with her. I'd freaked myself out overthinking it as usual. I felt so panicky and worried. Looking back, I don't know how I'd gotten myself in such a tizz. There was nothing spooky, gross or scary. It was just a person. Just a body. She manages everything so well. She really is inspirational. I admire her more than any other nurse I've met. If I had the choice, I'd want her or someone like her to care for me when I am dying. She makes it seem so normal. Death is normal. Inevitable. So calm. I've learnt such a lot from her. She really is special. She's my yardstick to measure others against and someone to aspire to myself. She always seems to have time. Gets things done but never sloppy or in a rush. Just keeps plodding steadily along.

And her jerk chicken! Love it love it love it.

18
BONFIRE NIGHT

"Last night I slept like a log. I woke up in the fireplace."
Tommy Cooper

Bonfire night was a warmly anticipated annual community event, organised by the Porters at St Luke's. They began collecting and piling up wooden pallets, old chairs, and tables in the middle of the green from the end of September. By November 5th, the pile was huge. All the patients, staff, friends, and families were invited. It was a popular date on the calendar.

People started arriving a little before 5pm. Families of all ages—granny, grandpa, aunts and uncles, parents with children walking, and babies in buggies—all wrapped up in hats, scarves, gloves, and warm coats.

The hospital kitchen staff served up burgers, hot dogs, soup, and cheese rolls at bargain prices that just covered costs. The delicious smell of fried onions and tangy minestrone soup drew the crowds, and there was a brisk trade in tomato sauce, brown sauce, and mustard.

The Guy Competition was always extremely popular, with a huge array of guys appearing. There were cartoon characters, local politicians, celebrities, and prime ministers, all made using old clothes stuffed with crumpled newspaper. Faces were cut from cardboard, stuck or painted on. It was extraordinary how lifelike some of them were. They arrived in wheelbarrows, prams, pushed, or proudly carried on the backs of their makers.

The judging was carried out by Keith, the Head Porter. Instantly recognisable, Keith was a large man, six foot five inches tall, with a shiny bald head and large nose. A bit of a 'jobs-worth,' Keith was opinionated, loud, but conscientious and keen for everyone to enjoy themselves safely. He liked being in charge and loved being the centre of attention. He enjoyed wearing a uniform, and on Bonfire Night he was in his element, in his black hat and yellow, fluorescent jacket with "Head Porter" printed in bold red letters on the back.

Keith was a bit of a rough diamond, but he was a decent family man who also volunteered for many good causes. He took his time swaggering slowly up and down the row of guys, nodding, smiling, and asking the makers about each one. He milked his moment of glory for all it was worth!

The winners of the Guy Competition that night were 'Laurel and Hardy,' made by the family of one of the charge nurses, who were delighted to be presented with the prize: a box of Maltesers and a voucher for a meal for four at a local pub, The Nags Head. Everybody cheered when Keith announced them as the winners.

The family were invited to be the first to toss Laurel and Hardy on the pile, and then Keith gestured for everyone else to throw their guys on too. A rush of people came forward, throwing their guys onto the wooden heap with little ceremony.

Keith then barked, "Okay everyone—back behind the rope, please. Back you go. Behind the rope. Thanks folks. Come on now, let's get this fire started!"

The other porters helped to usher the crowd away from the bonfire heap and behind the rope fence. Keith walked around the staked and roped circle, the boundary keeping people at a safe distance. When he was finally satisfied, the countdown began. The whole crowd joined in, shouting out loudly:

'10... 9... 8... 7... 6... 5...' Keith strolled towards the pile with Dave, his deputy. '... 4... 3... 2... 1...' He lit an oil-soaked rag and pushed it into a nook pre-prepared with dry paper and small kindling, then stepped back.

For a moment, it seemed the fire wasn't going to catch. We all held our breath, staring at the place Keith had lit. Then one small tongue of flame flickered out, followed by another, and another, until the pile was alight. The flames grew, the wood crackled and glowed, flames leaped higher and higher, warming the faces of the crowd. We cheered.

Engulfed by the flames, the sight of the guys' bodies burning was bizarre. Their stuffed paper heads and faces began melting and falling, dropping to the ground and sizzling on the grass.

Keith waited until the bonfire was fully alight and under control, then signalled to Dave. Together, they handed out long silver foil packets of sparklers to the children. Each foil packet contained five sparklers, and the children's eyes widened with excitement. Soon, the whole circle was alive with kids making spiral shapes and writing their initials with the glowing, sparkling sticks.

The children stared in amazement as each new sparkler fizzed to life. The spent sparklers were dropped into sand-filled tin buckets placed along the rope barrier.

Once again, Keith timed everything perfectly. As the sparklers fizzled out, he beckoned to Dave, and they approached the waiting line of fireworks. Keith lit each blue touchpaper with an electric lighter. Slowly, one by one, the rockets and Catherine wheels exploded into life, with chrysanthemums of stars and fiery comet balls trailing sparks as they zoomed skyward.

The watching crowd, heads tipped back, eyes fixed on the dark sky, emitted loud 'ooohs' and 'aaahs' as the big fireworks ignited, banging, popping, and fizzing with multicoloured lights and sparkles. The finale was a stunning sequence of bright aerial fireworks, fired in rapid succession.

Keith beamed as the show fell silent. The crowd clapped and cheered. We began to move slowly away from the fire, which had now burned down to a hot pile of glowing ashes. Everyone was happy and satisfied, having enjoyed another wonderful display.

As we left the green, the ladies who volunteered for the Friends of the Hospital handed out small bags of sweets to the children. Dolly mixtures, jelly tots, jellybeans, and sultanas were lovingly wrapped in pink and white striped paper bags. Tom, Lizzie and I enjoyed a happy evening together. They ate their treats as we walked home, while chatting excitedly about the fireworks.

Keith and Dave stayed until the bonfire was completely out, long after the last person had left. They pottered about in the darkness with their torches, picking up wastepaper, untying the rope barrier, and putting away the stakes and buckets of sand.

Once they were satisfied that the fire was safe to leave, Keith took out a hip flask of whiskey. He shared a tot with Dave, thanked him for his help, and shook his hand warmly. "Another year over, Dave. Best fireworks yet, I reckon". "You're right, Keith," Dave nodded. "Well done, mate. Cheers. No problem. See you tomorrow."

19
VALIUM - THE WARD CAT

"If a black cat crosses your path, it signifies that the animal is going somewhere."
Groucho Marx

Acacia Ward was a thirty-bed female geriatric ward, with a core team of dedicated, permanent staff who worked hard to enhance the lives of the patients. The patients had a range of physical illnesses and psychiatric conditions, and complex physical needs, including heart disease, hypertension, and congestive heart failure. Many suffered from arthritis and osteoporosis, which led to joint pain, stiffness, and an increased risk of fractures. There was also chronic obstructive pulmonary disease (COPD) and other respiratory issues, along with diabetes and its associated complications.

Many of the ladies were hard of hearing and had age-related impaired vision. Musculoskeletal problems and mobility impairments, such as difficulty walking or balance issues, were addressed through physical therapy and support. Mental health concerns included depression, anxiety, and conditions like Parkinson's disease, dementia, and Alzheimer's.

Acacia Ward had its own cat. A tabby of indeterminate age, breeding, or origin, she had wandered in one day, was fed by a kind nursing assistant, and decided to stay. When it became clear that she was staying, the staff named her—Valium.

Valium was a hefty cat, boasting a generously rounded physique, her body well-padded and soft to the touch. Her most striking feature was her thick, plush fur, marked with the classic tabby pattern—a mix of warm, earthy tones blending shades of brown, tan, and black in a striped or marbled design. The patterns created a unique mosaic that seemed to emphasise the cat's ample size.

Her feline face was broad and round, adorned with a pair of large, expressive eyes that exuded curiosity, contentment, and watchfulness. Her eyes were a captivating mix of green, amber, and gold, framed by soft, thick whiskers that twitched with each movement. Her nose was wide, with small ears in comparison to her round face.

Despite her size, she moved with a deliberate grace, her plump paws supporting her weight comfortably. A thick tail completed her visually appealing ensemble. Overall, this large, fat tabby radiated a sense of cosiness and contentment, inviting anyone to indulge in the pleasure of giving her an affectionate stroke or pet.

However, doing so was a mistake, as Valium was very choosy about who she allowed the honour of petting her, and she had a clear boundary when it came to physical contact. The cat would gracefully evade any attempts at stroking or petting, skilfully sidestepping eager hands.

When approached with outstretched fingers, Valium would subtly arch her back and emit a soft, warning growl—a clear signal that she preferred her own company. If the person didn't take the hint, Valium would hiss. She'd even been known to scratch or bite. It wasn't that she was unfriendly, rather that she cherished her autonomy and valued her personal space.

Valium enjoyed sharing the room with the ladies, but the touch of an unwanted hand was met with a gentle retreat and avoidance. It was as if Valium communicated, "I appreciate your presence, but let's keep a respectful distance."

The enigma of Valium added an intriguing dynamic to Acacia Ward. While some cats crave affectionate strokes and cuddles, Valium flourished in her own world of independence. She became a staff member not through physical touch but through the silent companionship she offered to those she chose.

Valium also had an uncanny ability to sense when someone needed comfort. If a patient was feeling down or stressed, she would nuzzle against them, offering a reassuring presence. Her loud purrs acted as a gentle remedy, calming frayed nerves and bringing a sense of tranquillity to the ward.

Staff either loved or loathed Valium. This was generally based on whether she chose to grace them with her presence and, of course, whether they liked cats or not.

Valium had her favourite staff. Those who loved her brought tins of cat food and treats to the ward to add to her store cupboard. They also pooled money to cover her vet bills and buy new beds and brushes for her.

Valium would fix those staff she loathed with a haughty stare, avoiding and ignoring them. Once she'd made up her mind about a person, she never changed it.

Her presence often caused tension and conflicting opinions among the staff. Those who disliked her argued that she posed an infection control risk, and that caring for her involved time and effort that should be dedicated to the patients. They also raised concerns that the presence of a cat could exacerbate health issues for certain patients or staff members.

Those who loved her maintained that she provided companionship and comfort, promoting emotional well-being among the patients and helping to reduce stress and anxiety. They cited studies suggesting that pet therapy with animals like cats can be beneficial in healthcare settings. Staff also argued that caring for a cat gave patients a sense of purpose and a reason to engage in daily activities.

So, having Valium wasn't always as positive as you might think. Her presence often sparked debate among the staff, and I overheard snippets of it when I worked a shift there. I'm much more of a dog lover, so she didn't affect me, and because I wasn't a permanent member of staff, I had no strong view about Valium either way.

What I did notice was that through the highs and lows, through staff changes and patient admissions, discharges, and deaths, Valium remained unfazed by any tensions, uninterested in staff opinion, haughty, hefty, and aloof.

Valium remained a constant. A smug constant.

20
NOT ALL CARERS CARE

"There is no rose without a thorn. But many a thorn without a rose."
Schopenhauer

There is a widespread belief that individuals in the medical professions are compassionate and dedicated to helping others, and generally, I think this is true. Many healthcare professionals are driven by a genuine desire to make a positive impact on their patients' lives, working tirelessly, often under immense pressure, to provide the best possible care.

However, healthcare is not immune to having its share of unscrupulous individuals. Some workers may be lazy, displaying a lack of motivation and dedication to their duties. Others can be unkind, showing little empathy or consideration for their patients' feelings and well-being. There are also those who are indifferent, treating their roles merely as jobs to fulfil their own needs, without any genuine concern for the people they are supposed to care for.

These negative traits can manifest in various ways, such as neglecting patients' needs, providing substandard care, or even engaging in unethical behaviour. Individuals like Trevor, Patricia, and Doctor White can undermine the trust and respect that the medical profession typically commands, highlighting the importance of maintaining high standards and accountability within the system. (*14)

Trevor

Trevor worked as a nursing assistant on Elm Ward, a mixed-sex long-stay ward at St Luke's. His presence evoked numerous reactions among the staff and patients alike. He was a figure of contrast and conflicting perceptions, stirring whispers of curiosity and concern in equal measure.

Most of his colleagues found him to be a reliable and compassionate nurse, a steady hand in times of need. They admired his dedication and commitment to his patients, seeing in him the embodiment of the caring spirit that defined their profession. To them, Trevor was an integral part of the team and a source of support and camaraderie.

But alongside these voices of admiration, there were whispers of unease. Rumours hinted that there was "something odd" about Trevor. Some staff were slightly unsettled by his presence, sensing a quality that defied easy explanation. They muttered words of caution and were wary of the mysteries that seemed to shroud his past.

Nearly all the patients greeted him with warmth and familiarity, their faces lighting up at the sight of him. Others, however, cast wary glances in his direction, their uneasiness tinged with a sense of apprehension.

A short, stocky man in his fifties, Trevor had an assortment of low-quality tattoos scattered across both forearms: a swallow, the word "Mum," a compass, and dolphins. Notably, the letters ACAB were inked on his knuckles.

Years of smoking and drinking during his younger years had made his voice gruff. Raised in a children's home and shuffled between foster families, Trevor was what some might call a "home boy," a man shaped by a childhood marked by transience and adaptation.

He was always on time, well presented, polite even. But there was something shifty about him. Nothing you could quite put your finger on. But there was something. Trevor got on with his work. He didn't stand out. He was just there, comfortable in the ward routine, knew his job, and got on with it. He didn't gossip about others. He talked to everyone on a superficial basis. He never got too friendly with anyone and rarely socialised on ward nights out. He kept to himself.

He was a member of the Sports and Social Club pool team and happily took part in matches against other clubs. He drank Coke or lemonade and paid for his own drinks, refusing to take part in rounds with the rest of the lads. He was a talented player, so no one minded.

The mystery surrounding Trevor unravelled when a young student nurse unintentionally stepped in. As I understand it, he'd accidentally left his coat at work after an early shift. Sean, a first-year student nurse, noticed this and, eager to lend a hand, offered to drop it off at Trevor's house while cycling past on his way home.

Trevor's front door was slightly ajar when Sean knocked on it, so he pushed it open further, calling out to Trevor as he did so. The door opened directly into the living room. Sean could see right through the house into the backyard, as the doors to the kitchen and outside were all open.

The living room was piled high with hospital-issued medical supplies: boxes holding bandages, syringes, gloves, masks, gauze, and wound care materials. Shelves contained disposable gloves, masks, goggles, and gowns. There were bottles of disinfectants, sanitisers, and cleaning solutions—all marked with a familiar yellow sticker reading "Property of St Luke's."

There were also boxes of hospital food: cereal, sugar, jam, marmalade, teabags, tins of beans and tomatoes, and industrial-sized packs of soap powder, shampoo, and bars of soap. Overall, the living room served as a storage space for hospital equipment and supplies, rather than as a typical domestic living area.

Sean's jaw dropped as he stood in Trevor's living room, just as Trevor re-entered through the kitchen door.

Both men froze, staring at each other in disbelief for a brief, tense moment. Sean quickly explained, "You left your coat at work, I was just dropping it off on my way home."

"Whatever you think you've seen, you haven't, lad," Trevor replied.

Feeling uneasy, Sean edged backwards towards the open door. With a sudden burst of panic, he ran, seized his pushbike, and bolted away, pedalling as if his life depended on it, with Trevor calling after him.

Unlike most of his fellow student nurses, Sean lived at home with his parents. He recounted the story to them both. His parents listened, and his father urged him to do "the right thing."

Sean made a phone call to the lead lecturer from the School of Nursing, who arrived at his home later that evening to take a formal statement.

Over the following weeks, the full scope of Trevor's side hustles became apparent. It turned out he'd been deceiving patients by accepting their money and placing bets on their behalf at the nearby bookmaker, Bob's Bookies. If they won, Trevor would claim a share of their winnings as well. If patients asked him to get shopping, there was always a mark-up "for going," and he always pocketed his share. He found ways to make money from every transaction.

Acting alone, he had set up a profitable enterprise by selling hospital supplies to neighbours and other care homes. Dealing only in cash, there was no trail, no record of his wheeling and dealing. He gave no details about any accomplices, staying adamant that he acted by himself.

While there was media attention, it soon died down when there was no evidence to suggest otherwise.

Trevor was an expert in patience and cunning. Skillfully flying under the radar, he had successfully siphoned off substantial sums of money over the years he spent at St Luke's. With his ill-gotten gains, he had paid off his mortgage, acquired a car of his own, and remained debt-free.

Additionally, he had prudently set aside funds in a modest savings account. Whispers circulated about a rumoured suitcase filled with cash hidden away somewhere, but no concrete evidence ever surfaced to validate such claims.

The question of how Trevor "got away with it" was complex and multifaceted. Legal processes must follow due diligence, and everyone is presumed innocent until proven guilty. Due to a lack of concrete evidence, Trevor received a minimal prison sentence for possession of stolen goods. On release, he moved to his holiday home in Marbella.

The patients Trevor had lied to and let down were shocked initially but soon forgot about him, as they were settled and cosseted in their lives at the hospital.

I never worked with him, but the staff who did said they were shocked at first, saying they always knew there was something "dodgy" about him. They then moved on with the treadmill of hospital care, forgetting about him too.

It was Sean who emerged as the primary casualty of the situation. The aftermath weighed heavily on him. Paranoia consumed him as he feared retaliation from Trevor. His once unwavering trust in the compassion of healthcare professionals was shattered, leaving him adrift in a sea of uncertainty. He ruminated over whether his father was right when he urged him to do "the right thing."

With each passing day, Sean grappled with a profound sense of disorientation. It was as if the very core of his identity had been stripped away, leaving him to navigate an unfamiliar and unsettling landscape. Unable to face going into the hospital, Sean was signed off sick, became depressed and withdrawn, and although Trevor never contacted him, he eventually gave up on his nursing career.

Patricia

Patricia, also known as Patsy or Pat (or, behind closed doors, in whispered tones, as "Fat Pat"), was an enrolled D-grade nurse on permanent night duty. She had the reputation of being cruel to the patients. Rumours circulated on the hospital grapevine regarding Pat's treatment of certain patients. It was said that she held favourites close while displaying animosity toward others.

Allegations suggested that she singled out individuals for unfair treatment—denying them nighttime hot drinks, administering excessive medication, pushing and shoving patients, turning them roughly in bed, delivering small pinches and punches, and neglecting to adjust room temperatures, leaving patients uncomfortably cold. She was also said to hook their nightclothes over the back of the toilet and subject them to unnecessary restraint, leaving them unattended for prolonged periods.

Staff were always cautious around Pat. A large, intimidating woman with short black hair and heavily mascaraed eyes, she had a harsh nature and was quick to criticise and belittle junior colleagues.

A bully by nature, it was impossible to raise concerns about her without solid evidence. There was so much hearsay and rumour, but no one ever felt confident enough to speak out.

Reluctance to raise concerns in healthcare environments stems from numerous factors. The hierarchical structure in healthcare settings often means that individuals in positions of authority hold significant power. This can create a culture of fear, where lower-ranking staff may be hesitant to speak up due to concerns about potential repercussions or backlash from those in authority.

Those who do speak out often fear retaliation or retribution. Sadly, this happened at St Luke's, where staff were frequently reprimanded, ostracised by colleagues, or even faced termination of employment. This fear prevented individuals from raising legitimate concerns about patient care or safety.

Staff worried that they would not be supported or taken seriously if they spoke up, leading to a culture of silence where problems went unaddressed. Healthcare professionals were also concerned about damaging their professional reputation or career prospects if they raised concerns about colleagues or systemic issues within the organisation.

And so, Pat got away with it.

Doctor White

Misconduct by a doctor in a psychiatric hospital can take various forms and can have grave consequences for patients and the reputation of the institution.

Dr White was a stalwart figure within the halls of St Luke's, his presence a constant source of reassurance for both staff and patients. With his wealth of experience, he seemed almost inseparable from the fabric of the hospital—as though he had always been there.

Over the years, Dr White had dedicated himself to the well-being of those under his care, earning the respect of his colleagues. Like many psychiatrists of his time, he possessed a distinctive eccentricity that set him apart. Amidst the bustling activity of ward rounds, he presented an enigmatic figure, seemingly lost in deep contemplation as he navigated the corridors of the minds of his patients. His outward demeanour suggested a serene absorption in the complexities of the human psyche, his half-lidded eyes adding to the aura of intense focus.

Attending his ward round was a rite of passage for us as students. He had a peculiar ritual during discussions. While ostensibly engrossed in conversation or observation, his hands would instinctively reach for the comforting weight of his teacup. Gripped firmly between his fingers, the cup became a vessel not just for tea but also for the intricacies of his ruminations. With meticulous care, he initiated a delicate ballet, stirring the contents of his cup in a mesmerising rhythm that seemed to mirror the cadence of his thoughts.

The implement he used for this ritual wasn't a conventional teaspoon but the pen that perpetually resided behind his ear. This unassuming tool served a dual purpose—both as a scribe for his insights, evident in his tiny case note writing, and as an instrument of communion with his elixir of contemplation: English breakfast tea.

With each stroke, he stirred not just the tea but also the depths of his own mind, coaxing forth revelations and insights that eluded the untrained observer. His unique style of thinking gave an interesting perspective to everyone attending. At times, he seemed brilliant, at others, a bit eccentric and off the wall.

Dr White's unconventional methods extended beyond the confines of the psychiatric ward. Care and compassion were interwoven with questionable practices.

Perhaps none of these were as controversial as his Sunday visits to patients' homes under the guise of "friendship." In a departure from traditional clinical boundaries, Dr White blurred the lines between professional obligation and personal connection, assuming the role of a trusted confidant rather than a mere psychiatrist.

With disarming sincerity, he would knock on the doors of his patients' homes, not as a doctor but as a friend, bearing gifts of companionship and solace.

During these clandestine visits, Dr White's true intentions became apparent. Far from a mere social call, these encounters served as a test of his patients' resilience in the face of adversity.

For those who had managed to resist the urge to self-harm, he offered a peculiar "reward"—the opportunity to accompany him on his leisurely Sunday strolls through the village streets, his canine companion Toby trotting faithfully alongside.

Beneath the veneer of benevolence lay troubling ambiguity. Critics questioned the ethics of his actions, arguing that his unorthodox methods risked blurring the boundaries between professional duty and personal favouritism. By bestowing rewards on those who refrained from self-harm, he created a system of incentives that could potentially undermine the integrity of therapeutic relationships.

These Sunday visits raised eyebrows among the staff, casting a shadow of doubt over his motivations. His Sunday rituals served as a reminder of the complexities and caution required in psychiatry, where the boundaries between care and control, compassion and coercion, could blur with unsettling ease.

The abrupt absence of Dr White from the on-call rota sent ripples of concern through the hospital. Whispers and speculation grew about his fate. With his name conspicuously absent, a veil of silence from senior management descended upon the staff, shrouding the truth behind a wall of secrecy.

Amidst the hushed murmurs and concerned glances, fear took root in the hearts of those who had relied on Dr White's presence. Had illness claimed him? Was he battling a terminal condition in solitude?

Despite the mounting apprehension among the staff, the managers remained tight-lipped, their lips sealed against enquiries. Behind closed doors, discussions unfolded in muted tones, guarded exchanges hinting at the gravity of the situation without revealing its true nature.

In the absence of concrete information, rumours flourished like weeds. Some speculated that he had embarked on a sabbatical or joined a research project in distant lands. Others whispered of darker possibilities—suggesting illness had confined him to a hospital bed or the sanctuary of his home.

The revelations surrounding Dr Archibald White sent shockwaves through the hospital community and beyond. As the veil of secrecy around his mysterious disappearance began to lift, a darker truth emerged, tarnishing the reputation of the once-respected psychiatrist.

The General Medical Council (GMC) panel's findings laid bare a troubling reality. Dr White, once regarded as a pillar of trust and compassion, had betrayed the very principles upon which his profession stood. In a case that sent ripples of disbelief through the community, it was revealed that he had exploited the vulnerability of a woman, identified only as Ms X, in a breach of trust that reverberated with profound implications.

Details emerged painting a picture of manipulation and deceit, as Dr White's purported acts of kindness were revealed as nothing more than a smokescreen for his ulterior motives.

The seemingly innocuous Sunday visits to patients' homes, under the guise of friendship and concern, took on a sinister hue as it became apparent, they were a means of exerting control and fostering dependence.

In the case of Ms X, Dr White's actions were deemed particularly deplorable, as he leveraged his position of authority to exploit her vulnerabilities for his own gratification. What had initially appeared as benevolent check-ins, rewards for abstinence from self-harm, and leisurely strolls with Toby, were now revealed as calculated manoeuvres designed to maintain a hold over his unsuspecting victim.

The panel heard troubling accounts of Dr White's misconduct, including engaging in sexual activity with patients during consultations and initiating an improper emotional and sexual relationship with a patient that spanned over fifteen years.

Ms X had sought treatment from Dr White for complex psychological issues. Shockingly, it was revealed that during one consultation between March and May 1984, Dr White locked the door of the consultation room and engaged in sexual activity with his patient. Ms X also disclosed that on several occasions they consumed alcohol together during consultations, and on four separate occasions, Dr White professed his love for her.

Despite the gravity of the allegations, Dr White—who had now reportedly retired from all medical practice—was conspicuously absent from the hearing and was not represented.

The revelations painted a disturbing picture of breach of trust and professional misconduct, raising serious concerns about ethical standards within the medical profession and the protection of vulnerable patients.

The ramifications of Dr White's betrayal reverberated far beyond the confines of the GMC panel's verdict. It cast doubt upon the integrity of the psychiatric profession.

Dr Archibald White's fall from grace served as a sobering reminder of the fragility of trust and the imperative of vigilance in safeguarding the well-being of vulnerable patients.

His name, once synonymous with compassion and care, was now tarnished by the stain of betrayal, leaving a legacy that would forever haunt St Luke's.

My Diary

Another shift with Fat Pat :) I've heard soooo many rumours about her. She doesn't do stuff when senior staff are around. If it's true what's said about her, she's obviously clever enough to know what she's doing and can stop doing it if she knows she's being watched. A bit creepy that.

I like to think I judge people based on my own experiences and what I see myself. I'd love to see Pat doing something first-hand.

I can honestly say that so far, I have never personally seen anything untoward. But there is a lot of gossip and speculation about Pat. I'll keep an eye out and do something about it if I see anything.

Or would I?? Would I though? Really? Would it even be worth it?

It's interesting because it reminds me of all the heated debates we had in our training lectures on governance, safety and institutionalisation.

1. There may be a keen sense of loyalty to colleagues or a desire to maintain harmonious team dynamics, which can make individuals reluctant to confront or challenge problematic behaviour or practice.

Bloody right! No one wants to be 'that person'. But perhaps we all should be???

2. Some individuals may feel that speaking out will not lead to any meaningful change or improvement, especially if they believe that management or the organisation is unlikely to act in response to their concerns.

Yes – I've heard lots about staff who have spoken up and then NOTHING has happened. Like that poor student Sean who found Trevor stealing all the hospital stuff. He left nursing. He did the right thing and spoke up. Then he wished he hadn't. Mum said that people talked about Dr White for years – they had their suspicions about him, but no one did anything.

3. *Addressing these barriers to speaking out requires fostering a culture of openness, transparency, and accountability within healthcare organisations. This includes providing avenues for anonymous reporting, offering support and protection for whistleblowers, encouraging constructive feedback, and actively addressing concerns raised by staff members. By promoting a culture where all voices are valued and respected, healthcare organisations can create safer and more supportive environments for both patients and employees.*

In an ideal world yes – reflecting on what I've seen though... that culture isn't there. No one really wants to deal with anything. Things get brushed under the carpet. Ignored. I don't know how it will change. People have their families and mortgages to think about.

4. *In environments where routines are tightly structured and responsibilities are standardised, it's not uncommon for both staff and patients to experience a sense of institutionalisation, disorientation, and detachment from the outside world. For hospital staff, the demands of patient care followed a predictable pattern, with each day much the same as the last. From medication rounds to patient assessments, charting, and administrative tasks, the routine of the afternoon shift can become so ingrained that it's easy to lose track of the outside world and the passage of time.*

Correct! Staff are more institutionalised than the patients!! It's like Groundhog Day. A never-ending cycle of tasks and responsibilities that blurs the distinction between one day and the next. There is a predictable monotony in the hospital. It's like another world. A secret world where stuff *happens behind closed doors. Stuff that isn't discussed outside. Hospital stuff.*

21
THE ECT SUITE

"If you're going through hell, keep going."
Attributed to Winston Churchill

Day Patient Unit, Mixed Sex, 20 Beds

St Luke's designated Electroconvulsive Therapy Suite, with twenty beds, conducted sessions on Monday, Wednesday, and Friday mornings, with up to twenty patients scheduled for treatment at each session.

I was rostered to work from 7:30 a.m. to 2:30 p.m. with the small, dedicated ECT team for three sessions that week (*15). My role involved various responsibilities before, during, and after the procedure to ensure the safety and well-being of the patients.

Before treatment, I would obtain informed consent from each patient, ensuring they fully understood the procedure and its implications. I then completed the assessment documentation, checking that they had abstained from food and drink beforehand, as per the guidelines. Patients were given prescribed pre-medication to help them relax and reduce anxiety. Once positioned comfortably on the treatment table, I would reassure them to alleviate any remaining discomfort or apprehension.

My other tasks included monitoring the patient's vital signs throughout the process, including heart rate, blood pressure, and oxygen saturation. I assisted the psychiatrist with administering muscle relaxants to prevent injury during the seizure, closely observing for any adverse reactions or complications.

During the procedure, the psychiatrist applied electrodes to the patient's head. A direct electrical current was passed between the electrodes for a few seconds, either from temple to temple (bilateral ECT) or from the front to the back of one side of the head (unilateral ECT), to induce a generalised seizure.

After the procedure, patients were moved to the recovery area, where post-ECT side effects such as confusion, headache, or nausea were carefully monitored and managed.

We would give patients a cup of tea and a biscuit—a reassuring break as they transitioned from the procedure to the recovery phase. At this time, we also documented their responses, reporting any adverse reactions or complications.

After the patients had left, we set about preparing the ECT suite for the next session. This included sanitising all equipment, thoroughly disinfecting surfaces, and meticulously sterilising the electrodes.

The beds were stripped and remade with fresh, crisp sheets, with a folded blue blanket placed at the foot of each bed. The blue and white curtains between beds were drawn back, creating an inviting and comfortable space ready for the next round of patients.

Once the suite was restored to its pristine state and the nursing staff were satisfied that everything was in order, we left the building at 2:30 p.m. sharp.

I enjoyed the calm atmosphere and the orderliness of the well-run, clean ECT suite. But as I went about my duties, I couldn't help but feel conflicted about the treatment itself.

On the one hand, I witnessed profound transformations in patients who had been catatonic or severely depressed, as they emerged from their fog and embraced life anew. Their recovery seemed nothing short of miraculous.

A good example was William, a man in his early seventies who had been admitted with catatonic depression. Catatonia is a neuropsychiatric syndrome characterised by motor disturbances, including immobility, mutism, rigidity, and unusual posturing, alongside typical depressive symptoms such as persistent sadness, low mood, and fatigue.

William had been unresponsive for hours, his body rigid and his face expressionless, experiencing profound psychomotor retardation. His family were beside themselves with worry, having watched their father deteriorate over a long period. Medication and psychotherapy had yielded no results, and ECT was seen as a last resort.

After just two sessions, William's progress was nothing short of remarkable. He emerged from the shadows, slowly reclaiming aspects of himself that had seemed lost. Within days, he began talking, eating, and walking again. His family were overjoyed. The change was extraordinary, a testament to the incredible impact of ECT on his life.

On the other hand, I had concerns about ECT's potential side effects, including memory loss and cognitive impairments. Critics argued that it was sometimes overused, with alternative treatments left unexplored. There were also ethical debates about administering ECT without the patient's full informed consent.

As I nursed the patients in the ECT suite, I understood that every decision carried weight, and every action had consequences. While I remained committed to providing compassionate care, navigating the ethical dilemmas of ECT made me feel uneasy at times.

Each day working in the unit forced me to confront the complexities of my profession. It wasn't easy.

My Diary

There's a lot to like about working in the ECT suite. The work is straightforward, the staff are efficient, and I love the clean, tidy, organised set-up. But it's repetitive, and you don't get much interaction with the patients.

That said—here's the biggie—I'm not sure about ECT. I couldn't work there full-time, but the occasional shift is fine. A week even. That's the joy of being a bank nurse!

I've seen ECT do incredible things. But I'm still not 100% comfortable with it. Would I have it myself? I don't know... Would I want anyone in my family to have it? Again, I'm not sure. If everything else had been tried, I suppose you'd have to give it a go.

22
AWOL – THE SEARCH

"The point is not what we expect from life, but rather what life expects from us."
Viktor Frankl

Occasionally, patients would go missing at St. Luke's. It wasn't uncommon for them to wander off and become lost in the maze of corridors, especially if they were confused or disoriented. Other times, they may have agreed to return at a specific time but failed to do so for a variety of reasons.

If a patient didn't return to the ward at the appointed time, staff would begin a diligent search, starting on the ward itself and then expanding to the area they were supposed to be in. A patient was deemed Absent Without Leave (AWOL) if, after a risk assessment, it was concluded that they had left the hospital without permission, failed to return after an approved leave, or had taken leave without permission from any place they were required to stay according to the conditions of their leave grant.

The uncertainty surrounding a missing patient would trigger a search effort, and if deemed necessary, the Nursing Officer in charge would initiate the Missing Persons Procedure. Working with the porters, the Nursing Officer would coordinate and direct the search team.

When the procedure was activated, a loud siren was sounded from the porters' lodge. Each ward and department promptly dispatched one staff member to the lodge to join the search team, which would then systematically search the hospital premises and surrounding areas for the missing patient.

To ensure an organised search, a comprehensive map of the hospital and its grounds was divided into a numbered and lettered grid. Each square on the grid was assigned to two staff members, who were equipped with torches, whistles, and fluorescent yellow jackets bearing numbers corresponding to the grid section they were tasked with searching. This system ensured thorough coverage and a swift response to any potential sightings or clues regarding the patient's whereabouts.

The procedure was highly effective, and staff executed their roles with efficiency and coordination under the guidance of the porters. Thanks to their teamwork, searches were generally successful, with most patients being located safe and sound. The operation was a testament to the organisation and professionalism of the hospital staff.

I was dispatched to a search one wintery night at 7 p.m. when the siren sounded. It was cold, dark, and windy outside. I was assigned to search Area D4, a wooded patch on the edge of the cricket pitch at the front of the hospital. My search partner was Chris, a staff nurse from Maple Ward. We'd worked together before, so no introductions were needed, and we set off into the darkness with our torches.

Wrapped up in coats and our fluorescent jackets, each pair of searchers left to scour their designated area. We were informed that the missing person was a seventeen-year-old boy last seen at The Oaks, the Adolescent Unit. This was his first admission following a drug-induced psychosis. He was last seen wearing jeans, white trainers, a black INXS T-shirt, and a black hoodie. His name was Ricky.

"How's life?" asked Chris as we trudged across the cricket pitch.

"Good, thanks. How about you? Are you and Lesley still thinking of taking a year out to go travelling?"

"Yeah, we've saved enough. We'll go in the next three months or so. Really looking forward to it. We want to be somewhere warm, away from this cold. It's bloody bleak, eh?" said Chris, pulling his hood tighter against the wind.

We'd reached our designated area and began scanning it with our torches, looking for any sign of movement or clues that could lead us to Ricky. The wooded area was dense, and the darkness added an eerie feel to our search.

We took turns calling out, "Ricky! Can you hear us?"

In the distance, we could hear other teams calling out as they searched their own areas.

"Any idea how long he's been missing?" My breath was visible in the cold air.

"I think they said about three hours," Chris replied, his voice tinged with concern. "Hopefully, we can find him quickly."

We pressed on through the woods, our footsteps crunching softly on the fallen leaves and twigs. The beams from our torches flitted across the trees, casting long shadows that seemed to reach out towards us.

We searched Area D4 as thoroughly as possible, sweeping our torch beams over the ground and up the trees.

"Anything?" I whispered.

"Nothing," Chris responded. "Shall we head back?"

"Yeah, I don't think he's here," I agreed, feeling disappointed.

I shouted again, "Ricky! Ricky! Can you hear us?"

As we turned to head back, a high-pitched whistle pierced the night from somewhere to our right. We exchanged a look, eyes wide with unspoken understanding, and then we both ran towards the sound.

Guided by the whistle, we navigated the woods, our torches cutting through the darkness. Each step brought us closer to the source.

As we approached, the whistle grew louder. We soon saw a gathering of staff beneath the trees, their fluorescent jackets casting an eerie glow.

"What's happening?" Chris asked, his voice a mix of concern and curiosity.

The Nursing Officer, his face sombre, gestured upwards. We followed his gaze and gasped.

Suspended by a rope, Ricky's limp body swung gently from a tree, his arms and legs hanging lifeless. He was dressed just as described: jeans, a black hoodie, and white trainers. The grim reality of the situation hit us all at once.

Nobody spoke.

As we waited in silence for the police, fire brigade, and ambulance to arrive, tears streamed down my cheeks. I was in shock. Though I'd heard of such tragedies, seeing it firsthand was mind-blowing. Glancing at my colleagues, I saw the same shock mirrored in their faces.

When the emergency services arrived, the Nursing Officer asked the two staff who had found Ricky to remain, while the rest of us were dismissed. Deflated, we returned to our wards to share the tragic news. It was a sad end to the day for the entire hospital.

The Oaks Adolescent Psychiatry Unit stood as a separate enclave within the sprawling grounds of St Luke's, distinct yet connected to the hospital. Surrounded by tall iron fences, the unit exuded an air of containment and protection. Despite its institutional appearance, efforts were made to soften the harshness of the surroundings with flower beds and shrubs lining the pathways.

Inside, the corridors echoed with the subdued hum of activity. The walls, painted in muted tones, displayed vibrant artwork by the young residents, showcasing great creativity and expression despite their internal struggles. Each bedroom was sparse yet functional, equipped with a bed, a small desk, and a chair, giving each young person a private place for rest and introspection.

The communal areas were gathering spaces for therapeutic activities and group sessions. The adolescents came together under the guidance of the multidisciplinary team to explore their emotions, share experiences, and learn coping strategies.

During the day, the adolescent unit whirred with activity, a hive of therapeutic interventions and educational endeavours designed to support the mental and emotional growth of its young residents. Therapy sessions included individual and group therapy and provided a safe space for the adolescents to explore their inner struggles and develop coping skills. Educational classes offered a sense of structure and purpose, empowering residents with knowledge and skills to navigate life beyond the unit. Sports, arts and crafts, and outdoor activities, encouraged social interaction and physical well-being.

Underlying the veneer of productivity and positivity, lay an undercurrent of pain and turmoil. The adolescents within the unit carried the weight of their past experiences and current struggles, their emotions often simmering just below the surface. The atmosphere could shift from calm to chaotic in the blink of an eye, as emotions ran high, and tempers flared.

The staff of The Oaks were not only highly trained professionals but also a deeply committed team of individuals with a profound understanding of the fragility of youth and the complexities of mental health. They navigated the challenges of their work with empathy and resilience, providing unwavering support and guidance to their charges. Staff worked tirelessly to create a nurturing environment where adolescents could heal and grow.

The news about Ricky hit them hard. He'd apparently enjoyed a weekend leave with his parents and two sisters, and according to his parents, it went smoothly.

They ate Sunday lunch as a family, during which Ricky was lively, cheerful, and engaged in conversation with his siblings. They returned him to The Oaks as scheduled at 4pm, with no worries or concerns about his well-being.

Ricky had signed in, had a brief friendly chat with one of the staff then went to his room to unpack. Staff couldn't recall any further sightings of him afterward. During supper roll call, his absence was noted, prompting a search of The Oaks. When he couldn't be found, the duty nurse manager was informed of his disappearance and the Missing Persons Procedure was instigated.

The news of Ricky's death stirred up a frenzy in both local and national media, some handled the sensitive subject matter with compassion and respect, while others sensationalised the tragedy, seeking to apportion blame and adding to the family's anguish. Intrusive inquiries, speculative reporting, and the invasion of privacy compounded their trauma, making it difficult for them to mourn in peace and find closure.

The family were left wrestling with the unimaginable loss of Ricky, compounded by the relentless torment of wondering what they or The Oaks could have done differently to prevent such a tragic outcome. Shock, disbelief, anger, and profound sadness created a landscape of pain. The void left by his death was a constant reminder of his young life cut short and so many dreams left unfulfilled.

The Oaks staff felt the impact of Rickys suicide intensely. Despite their best efforts to provide care and support, feelings of guilt, self-doubt, and helplessness remained. The team questioned whether they missed warning signs or failed to intervene effectively, struggling with a profound sense of responsibility for the tragedy that unfolded under their watch. His loss weighed heavily on them.

While the unpredictable nature of Ricky's suicide absolved them of any blame, the hospital and the team encountered increased scrutiny and pressure to review protocols and procedures to avert similar incidents in the future.

It was a painful time for everyone.

My Diary

What a shit night. A shitty, shitty night. That poor boy. My heart goes out to him, his family, and everyone at The Oaks. They're such a good team. Why though? Why did he do it? WTF???

I couldn't believe it. For a minute, I thought it was a prank—like he'd start laughing and say, "Hahaha! Got ya!" I can't get the image out of my mind. It's really freaked me out. I keep thinking about the smell of the woods and his little limp body, just hanging there.

If that was Tom... I can't even think about it. So sad. What a waste of life. Over before it even began. I'll never forget it. Bloody awful. But why? It's so final. There's no coming back from it.

And no one asks how the staff are! Not one person has asked how I feel after seeing that. It's just another day at the hospital, par for the course. The team at The Oaks are devastated. It's hard to get your head around it. So young. Such a pointless tragedy.

23
THE OUTING

"Do not adjust your mind, the fault is in reality."
R. D. Laing

Linden Ward. Long Stay. Mixed Sex. 28 Beds.

St. Luke's was fortunate to have two ten-seater minibuses, generously donated by the Friends of St. Luke's. These minibuses were invaluable for organising outings and drives for the patients. The system was simple but effective: wards could book the buses for a designated time slot to take patients on various excursions. Whether it was a trip to the seaside, a visit to a café or country pub for lunch, a picnic in the countryside, or a tour of a local attraction, the minibuses offered patients the chance to explore and enjoy new experiences beyond the hospital walls.

The outings were both recreational and therapeutic, offering patients the opportunity to socialise, connect with nature, and engage in activities that promoted their well-being. The minibuses provided a temporary escape from the hospital environment, allowing patients and staff alike to enjoy the outside world.

Working the mid-shift on Linden Ward, a unit for individuals aged 30 to 65 with severe and enduring mental illnesses, I had been tasked with overseeing the well-being of the patients chosen for today's outing. I was keenly aware of the added responsibility.

Linden Ward operated with a ratio of one staff member to every three patients during outings, reflecting the level of care required for these individuals. The protocol stressed the importance of close supervision and support, especially outside the ward, where risks could be heightened.

Reg, the minibus driver for Linden Ward outings, was a quiet, reserved gentleman who approached his job with great care. Behind the wheel, he navigated the roads with a steady hand, always prioritising the safety of his passengers. Though he didn't engage much in conversation, his presence was reassuring, and we all knew we were in capable hands.

His cautious approach and dedication made him an integral part of the Linden Ward team.

The plan for today was a drive along the coast, giving six patients from Linden Ward the chance to enjoy the scenery and fresh sea air. The three men and three women would stop for lunch at *The White Swan*, followed by a leisurely drive back, with a possible stop for ice cream and a paddle in the sea, depending on the weather and time.

My colleague Vicky and I phoned ahead to arrange the meal choices and confirm our arrival time. We were greeted warmly at *The White Swan* and shown to a quiet table. Reg chose to stay in the minibus, smoking his pipe, enjoying his packed lunch, and listening to the radio.

I couldn't help but notice the contrast between our patients and the other patrons enjoying their bar meals. The men, dressed in their hospital-issued tweed jackets, shirts, and ties, and the women in floral polyester dresses and cardigans, stood out. They looked out of place in the pub, and I felt a pang of empathy for them. Outside their comfort zone of the hospital, their unsure glances sought reassurance from us, and their unfamiliarity with the setting was obvious.

Despite the initial awkwardness, Vicky and I made sure to provide reassurance, helping them navigate the unfamiliar surroundings and ensuring that everyone felt included. They savoured their bar meals—scampi and chips, gammon and pineapple, steak pie—and engaged in light conversation. We made sure they were happy and comfortable.

After lunch, we returned to the minibus. Reg, always watchful, noted that the skies had remained clear, so we decided to stop at the beach. The car park next to the beach had stone steps leading down to the shore. Pebbles crunched underfoot as we made our way towards the sand and sea.

Several patients quickly removed their shoes and socks, venturing to the water's edge. Their laughter mingled with the sound of the waves. Vicky and I took turns paddling with them, enjoying this simple pleasure away from the confines of the hospital. Reg fetched ice creams while we helped dry the patients' feet.

Soon, we were all sitting on the beach, enjoying 99s with flakes. Contentment washed over us as we relaxed in the warmth of the sun and the gentle sea breeze. Reg, sporting a knotted handkerchief on his head, licked his ice cream, much to the amusement of the group. It was a picture-perfect moment.

Then, chaos descended. From nowhere, a flock of more than ten seagulls launched a surprise attack, dive-bombing us in their audacious quest for our ice creams. They swooped and squawked, snatching at our cones with astonishing speed. The air was filled with cries and squeals as we tried to fend them off.

Reg, jumping up and down, waved his handkerchief-clad head and shouted, "Shoo! Shoo away!"

The patients' reactions varied. Two of the women clung to each other, their faces etched with fear. Another woman, however, laughed heartily, clapping her hands in delight. One man remained calm, pulling his jacket over his head and continuing to eat his ice cream under its shelter, while another made a beeline for the safety of the minibus. A third joined Reg in his frantic dance, mimicking his shouts of "Shoo away!" as they tried to chase off the seagulls.

The attack was over as quickly as it had begun. Once the seagulls realised there was no more ice cream to be had, they flew off, leaving us ruffled but relieved.

"Back to the bus!" bellowed Reg. We hurried back to the car park, where the sixth patient had been patiently waiting.

We checked in with each patient as they climbed aboard.

"All okay?"

"That was quite something, wasn't it?"

"Blinking seagulls!"

Settling into our seats, we fell into a comfortable silence as Reg drove us steadily back to St. Luke's. As we travelled, I reflected on the day, particularly on the varied reactions to the seagull attack. It was a reminder of how individual differences—personality, past experiences, and emotional states all play a role in shaping how we respond to situations. The diverse responses of the patients were a clear demonstration of the complexity of human behaviour. We'd all experienced the same situation but our reactions were different.

Back at Linden Ward, the atmosphere buzzed with excitement as one of the female patients, who had enjoyed the seagull incident so much, animatedly recounted the day's events to the other patients and staff. I overheard her repeatedly using the word "squabble."

"It was such a squabble! I've never seen anything like it. I loved it!" she exclaimed. "And Reg! Oh, Reg, with his hanky!"

Intrigued, I asked, "What do you mean by 'squabble'? There wasn't an argument. Who was squabbling?"

She looked at me with disdain. "No one was squabbling, nurse. For your information, a group of seagulls is called a squabble. I would've thought even *you* would know that."

Her tone was dripping with condescension. "Don't they teach you anything at St. Luke's School of Nursing?"

With that, she turned on her heel and walked off, leaving me speechless.

"Well," I said, blushing with embarrassment, "you learn something new every day."

I smiled sheepishly at the staff. "That certainly put me in my place."

My Diary

What a belter of a day! Squabbling seagulls, ice cream mayhem on the beach—what an outing! You couldn't make it up! Reg, flapping his hanky—I've never seen him so flustered. I'll definitely think twice before volunteering for another trip. It's a huge responsibility. And I got well and truly put in my place! Who knew a group of seagulls is called a squabble? That'll teach me to open my mouth without thinking. She was sharp as a tack. I deserved it.

24
THE FYSHE

"A man's true character comes out when he's drunk."
Charlie Chaplin

The village pub stood at the junction at the bottom of the hill leading to St. Luke's and the road into the village. The weathered exterior boasted a timber-framed structure, with dark beams and buff-coloured paintwork, adding to its aged appearance. Above the entrance, a crooked wooden sign proudly displayed a picture of a fat blue and green fish, and the pub's name was faded but still legible: *The Fyshe.*

On one side of the entrance was the "beer garden," which was little more than a scruffy tarmacked square. A mismatched arrangement of old plastic and wooden chairs dotted the area, with a few picnic tables offering a place for patrons to enjoy the fresh air or have a smoke. Cigarette butts littered the ground, and patches of weeds sprouted defiantly through cracks in the car park, giving the place a neglected air.

Crossing the threshold, it felt as though time had stood still. The low ceilings had exposed wooden beams adorned with green hops, their delicate leaves and tendrils creating a verdant canopy overhead. They cast dappled shadows across the worn wooden tables below. The crooked walls were adorned with faded photographs of the village, and shelves were filled with ancient pottery tankards and leather-bound books.

At the far end of the pub, a roaring fireplace gave off woodsmoke and crackling flames, casting a flickering, smoky glow across the room. The atmosphere exuded a distinct rustic charm that came from years of wear and tear. The carpets, faded from foot traffic, bore the marks of countless spilled beers, and the faint scent of cigarettes still lingered. Despite its shabby appearance, *The Fyshe* remained popular with its regular patrons—staff and patients from the hospital, as well as locals from the village—who cherished its lived-in feel.

The furnishings showed their age, with slightly wobbly tables and mismatched chairs that creaked with every movement, their surfaces etched with the marks of many conversations and spilled drinks. Behind the bar, shelves were lined with bottles whose labels were faded by time, while the taps boasted a choice of beers from local breweries. The old bartender moved with ease amidst the clutter, expertly pouring drinks while engaging patrons in friendly banter.

Whether it was a sporting event, a popular game show, or the evening news, the television behind the bar was always on, its flickering images casting a soft glow over the pub. Mounted securely on the wall, it served as a focal point for those gathered around the bar, their attention alternating between lively conversation and whatever was happening on screen.

The Fyshe was rarely quiet. It usually buzzed with people and energy. The jukebox, standing in the corner, spun a web of nostalgia, filling the air with beloved classics. Despite the occasional crackle and pop from its aged speakers, its eclectic playlist transported patrons to a bygone era of timeless hits and unforgettable melodies.

From Tracy Chapman's soulful crooning to the infectious rhythms of The Beatles and The Police, each song evoked memories of days gone by. When the familiar chords of A-ha's *Take on Me* filled the room, smiles spread across the faces of those gathered, heads nodding and eyes closing, as they were instantly transported back to carefree nights.

The Fyshe was more than just a pub; it was the heart of our village and a cherished gathering place for both locals and hospital staff. Many a memorable night out began or ended there, its doors always open to those seeking friendship and connection.

The pub hosted everything from lively hen and stag nights filled with laughter to bingo nights buzzing with anticipation. Quiz nights tested patrons' knowledge, and christenings, weddings, and wakes were celebrated with equal parts joy and solemnity.

I had a fondness for *The Fyshe*. It felt comfortable and familiar. I celebrated my twenty-first birthday and my own hen night there and attended countless other parties and events. My grandmother's wake had been held in that very bar, and I imagine my parents' and mine would be too.

25
NIGHTINGALE HOUSE & CAVELL HOUSE

"Service to others is the rent you pay for your room here on Earth."
Muhammad Ali

The Nurses Homes. Mixed sex. 65 beds.

St Luke's had two nurses' homes situated in the grounds of the hospital. They provided mixed-sex, single-room accommodation for sixty-five staff. Nightingale House and Cavell House were named after the pioneers Edith Cavell and Florence Nightingale, in tribute to their contributions to the field of nursing and healthcare. (*16)

Both houses were constructed from red brick in the same style as St Luke's. Nightingale, the larger of the two houses, was situated above St. Luke's School of Nursing at the back of the hospital. Its location above the school provided convenient access for the forty nursing students and hospital staff living there. Cavell was a smaller standalone building, on a small side road off the main driveway up to the hospital, housing a further twenty-five staff.

The individual rooms in both houses were compact and modestly furnished, with a single bed, built-in wardrobe, chest of drawers, a small sink and mirror, and a desk. Communal areas were provided for socialising and relaxation. On the ground floor, was a television lounge and a smaller quiet lounge with comfortable seating and shelves with books and board games. Both houses had a communal laundry room with large stainless-steel sinks, washing machines, and tumble dryers. On each floor, there was a small, basic, shared kitchen where nurses could prepare meals.

Access to the buildings was limited to key holders only, and there were protocols in place to ensure the safety of the residents, especially during late-night shifts or emergencies.

As far as I knew, almost everyone got along. Like any community, discord occasionally reared its head, casting a shadow on the house. The rifts were usually caused by thoughtless individuals who, in their haste or neglect, left chaos in their wake. The kitchen would sometimes bear the scars of hurried meals, with dirty dishes piled high and countertops cluttered with sloppy remnants of cooking adventures. Bathrooms and showers would occasionally fall victim to neglect, their users leaving scum and hair behind for others to clean up. The communal spaces, intended for relaxation, would sometimes resemble a battlefield strewn with forgotten glasses, abandoned bottles, crisp packets, and takeaway boxes.

Despite the occasional skirmish and argument, the residents managed to coexist peacefully, agreeing that communal living wasn't always easy. Most staff moved out after a couple of years anyway. They moved on to new jobs in other hospitals or rented or bought their own homes in the village or city.

The atmosphere of the houses was always busy, with the comings and goings of staff creating a perpetual hum, regardless of the hour. With most of the residents being single, the air was often charged with the energy of romance and sexual relationships, social gatherings, and alcohol-fuelled parties. Laughter and music spilled from the rooms, and doors and windows were often left open, inviting colleagues to call in.

Mrs. Fothergill

Mrs. Marion Fothergill, a figure known as the 'house mother,' occupied an office on the ground floor of Nightingale House. Her role encompassed various responsibilities, including overseeing the maintenance of the houses, addressing inquiries from residents, and attending to their needs. She was a central point of contact, ensuring that both houses ran smoothly and that the residents felt supported and cared for during their stay.

She welcomed each new resident personally, ensuring their smooth transition into their new living quarters. She meticulously demonstrated the functionality of the cupboards and drawers, opening and closing each one to show their usefulness.

Before entrusting new staff with the key to their room, Mrs. Fothergill delivered a pep talk emphasising the importance of keeping quiet, respecting others, and not allowing 'overnight visitors.'

(The rule about overnight visitors was totally disregarded. Nightingale and Cavell rooms brimmed with secrets and stories of relationships that flourished and failed. A great deal happened within those walls!)

She missed nothing. She knew every resident by name and knew everything that went on. Exuding an aura of high tension, she briskly traversed the hospital corridors and houses, each step imbued with determination. Always in a rush and 'frightfully busy' all the time, she brooked no interference, and her demeanour radiated fierceness. If anyone dared to call her Marion, she would fix them with an icy glare and pointedly reply, "Excuse me. My name is Fothergill. Mrs. Fothergill to you."

The Baked Potato

I continued living at home with Tom and Lizzie during my training, but I spent a fair amount of time in Nightingale and Cavell, popping in for a coffee and chat, studying, partying, and sometimes staying over with one of my peers if Joe had the children.

One evening, at about 9pm, Sharon and I were sitting in the quiet lounge having a coffee and discussing an upcoming exam when we heard a commotion upstairs. Sharon listened for a while at the bottom of the stairs. Someone was shouting, running along the corridor, and banging on doors.

"Come on! Who's got it? I don't f...ing believe it! If I find you, look out! You cheeky bloody sods! Come on, I'm not laughing. Where is it? It's not on!"

We went upstairs to find out what was going on, discovering that Derek, a student nurse a couple of groups behind us, was the source of the racket.

"What's up, Derek?" enquired Sharon.

"I'll tell you what's up—some cheeky git has stolen my baked potato. I left it baking in the oven, came back forty minutes later, and it was GONE! Gone!! Can you fecking believe it! I'm bloody wild! It's not on!! Thieving GITS!" he yelled down the corridor. There was no answer. The doors to every room were closed.

Derek had obviously had a few pints at The Fyshe, come home feeling peckish, shoved a potato in the oven, and someone—who probably also felt peckish—had stolen it.

"Bloody starving I am! Hank Marvin! That was my last spud. I've got nothing else to eat! CAN YOU HEAR ME? You thieving sods! It's not on!"

"Derek! Derek!" hissed Sharon, "Be quiet. You're not going to find it now. They'll have eaten it. I've got some cereal if you want some?"

"Cereal?" snapped Derek sarcastically, then paused, looking thoughtful.

"What sort?"

"Coco Pops."

"You got any milk?"

'Yes. Loads," said Sharon, trying not to laugh as Derek swayed gently, trying to calm down.

"Okay then," he slurred.

Sharon went to her room and prepared a generous serving of Coco Pops, topped up with milk from the carton on her outside window ledge. (Most of the staff kept their milk here to avoid it being taken from the communal fridge). By then, Derek was perched on the edge of his bed, and she presented the bowl to him. Without hesitation, he accepted the offering, his hunger evident as he wolfed it down.

Sharon told me that food disappearing in the houses was quite common. We acknowledged the financial constraints faced by everyone, grappling with the challenges of making ends meet on the modest income of a student nurse. To safeguard their food, many resorted to storing their provisions within the confines of their rooms.

The theft of a baked potato from the oven was unusual, though. The audacity of such a theft left us both baffled. Perhaps someone else had come back from the pub, felt peckish, had no food, and decided to help themselves? A slice of bread or a handful of pasta was one thing. But a baked potato? We both agreed with Derek—it wasn't on.

Uncle Owen

The parties at Nightingale and Cavell were legendary for those of us who were fortunate enough to attend. Among the numerous memorable gatherings, one stood out: a lavish fancy dress affair to celebrate Robert's 30th birthday. Robert, a member of S Group, was a jovial student who loved dressing up and had an infectious knack for persuading others to join in.

Robert set the bar high with his elaborate ensemble, dressed as 'The King of Wales'—a dazzling tribute to his Welsh heritage, complete with a bright daffodil-yellow boiler suit, a white and green cloak adorned with red dragons, and a glittering golden crown studded with multi-coloured glass stones.

From medieval knights and fairytale princesses to eccentric steampunk inventors and glamorous Hollywood stars, the party was a kaleidoscope of creative costumes and imaginative characters. On this occasion, the rest of S Group embraced a playful theme, transforming ourselves into a riotous congregation of tarts and vicars, each bringing our own unique interpretation to the theme. The sight of so many tarts and vicars mingling amidst the fantastical backdrop of the party added an extra dynamic to the already vibrant atmosphere.

The Fyshe was the starting point for the festivities. It was buzzing with life, the vibrant costumes adding to the excitement. As the night progressed and spirits soared, our merry band of partygoers, high on life and alcohol, embarked on a joyous, wobbling procession up the winding drive to Cavell, where the celebrations continued well into the night.

Robert had transformed the lounge into a sea of yellow paper chains, streamers, and balloons, creating a crazy atmosphere of festive cheer. Adding to the jovial ambience was one of the hospital chefs, a close friend of Robert's and a fellow teammate on the hospital football team. Their shared passion for the game had forged a strong bond between them, and they now united their talents to ensure the party was a resounding success.

Towering stacks of golden buns, sizzling burgers, and hotdogs awaited the revellers, who now had the munchies, and we launched ourselves at the food with glee. There were crates of beer and lager, and on the hob in the kitchen stood a large steel saucepan bubbling with a concoction of fruity punch, inviting the guests to partake.

As the night wore on and the festivities reached a crescendo, we gathered around the makeshift buffet, indulging wholeheartedly. Music boomed, and the lounge buzzed with laughter, chatter, singing, and dancing. Friends old and new mingled, our spirits buoyed by the occasion. I was having the best time. Loving life. Drunk, but in a good way, I danced and chatted with everyone.

At two in the morning, a green Morris Minor van arrived. Robert had clearly been expecting it, and when he spotted it, he ushered us outside into the car park at the back of the house, which looked out over empty fields.

"Come on! Everyone outside! Come on, come, and see this!"

The driver of the van emerged, an old fellow clad in a shabby tweed suit, wellington boots, and a worn flat cap perched on his head. With deliberate steps, he made his way towards Robert, extending a weathered hand in greeting before proceeding to unlock the back doors of the van.

"Stand back!" he commanded, his voice carrying a sense of authority born from years of experience. With practiced ease, he reached into the depths of the van, emerging with a wooden crate adorned with an eclectic array of fireworks, secured in place with gaffer tape.

"Stand back! Stand back!" he repeated urgently, his tone leaving no room for hesitation. Ignoring the curious glances of onlookers, he swiftly ignited the fuse, setting in motion a chain reaction of explosive brilliance.

Instantly, the night sky was ablaze with colour and light as the fireworks erupted into a dazzling display that lasted only a couple of minutes. We gasped and cheered; our faces illuminated by the multicoloured lights dancing overhead.

The old chap's expertly orchestrated pyrotechnic spectacle unfolded before our eyes, a fitting crescendo to an unforgettable evening of celebration.

Show over, he lifted the crate back into the van, shook Robert's hand again, and slowly drove off down the drive. It was a surreal scene.

"What just happened?" inquired a perplexed medieval knight.

"That was fantastic!" exclaimed a fairytale princess, her eyes sparkling with drunken wonder.

Standing nearby, the unlikely duo of Mickey Mouse and Charlie Chaplin stood in awe, their mouths agape in astonishment at the spectacle they had just witnessed.

"Who the hell was that?" queried one of the many vicars, his confusion evident amidst the jubilant atmosphere.

Two of us tarts shook our heads in disbelief, grinning drunkenly up at the sky.

"That," declared Robert the King of Wales, with unmistakable pride, "was my Uncle Owen."

At the mention of Uncle Owen's name, the whole group erupted into a chorus of laughter and cheers, raising our glasses in a spontaneous toast to the pyrotechnic mastermind whose surprise fireworks display had left us all spellbound.

"To Uncle Owen!" we cheered, our voices echoing into the night as we celebrated the unexpected delight he had bestowed upon us.

"Uncle Owen!"

Mrs. Fothergill's Office

Mrs. Fothergill took the opportunity to take a break and left to visit her sister for two weeks. She spent a busy month beforehand ensuring that all was in order, informed all the residents by posting a handwritten note under each door, leaving specific instructions with the cleaning team for the two houses as she left.

During our lunchtime study block at St Luke's School of Nursing, Johann and Kate from S Group noticed that Mrs. Fothergill had inadvertently left her office window slightly ajar. Although they didn't mention it at the time, after a couple of beers together later that evening, they schemed to 'visit' the office under the cover of darkness the next night.

They both lived at Cavell House, and the full moon lit their path as they walked up the hill. Slightly inebriated, they tittered as they made their way around the back of Nightingale House. The window was still ajar. Johann pulled the window wide open, hoisted himself up and into the office, then leant out to help Kate.

They exchanged glances filled with tension and mischief in the semi-darkness, unable to believe they had successfully infiltrated Mrs. Fothergill's inner sanctum.

"Now what?" whispered Kate.

Johann walked slowly and purposefully around the office, touching nothing but looking closely at everything. A wide grin spread slowly across his face.

"Don't you think, Kate," he said, his eyes twinkling, "that the desk would look better over there? And that picture would look better over there..."

Kate caught on to his plan quickly.

Together, they meticulously rearranged every aspect of the room, shifting furniture, adjusting pictures, clocks, and photographs until the office bore little resemblance to its previous state.

Exhausted from their efforts, sweat glistening on their foreheads, they stepped back to admire their handiwork with a sense of satisfaction.

"We deserve a pint," said Kate.

"The Fyshe?" asked Johann.

"Certainly, mon vieux," smiled Kate.

At The Fyshe, they agreed to tell no one about their escapade. Grinning conspiratorially, they made their way back to Cavell and said nothing.

Ten days passed before Mrs. Fothergill finally returned from her holiday. Keen to get back to business and anticipating a pile of messages, she turned the key and pushed open the door to her office. Her anticipation quickly turned to shock as she stepped inside. Nothing was damaged, everything was tidy and in order, but her office was completely different.

She stood frozen in the doorway, her breath caught in her throat. Breaking the silence, she let out an ear-piercing wail of disbelief.

"Whooooooo has done this? Who...?"

Her voice, filled with a mix of horror and indignation reverberated off the walls. With adrenaline coursing through her veins, she wasted no time. She rushed to locate the cleaning team, her steps urgent and determined. She frog marched them all swiftly to her office, her eyes scanning their faces for any sign of guilt as she fired questions at them.

Satisfied that they knew nothing of the disturbance, she wasted no time in seeking out the Nurse in Charge. Bursting into the back office, she recounted the shocking scene, her voice trembling with anger and disbelief.

Mrs. Fothergill's quest for answers did not end there. With fiery determination, she confronted the porters and the Head of the School of Nursing, demanding explanations and accountability.

Word of the disturbance spread like wildfire through the hospital grapevine, gossip and speculation swirling in its wake. The corridors buzzed with the news about Mrs. Fothergill's office, leaving everyone to wonder: who did it?

Johann and Kate maintained their silence, choosing not to divulge their secret to anyone. They were both taken aback by the uproar their seemingly harmless joke had caused, and a sense of unease crept over them as they contemplated the potential repercussions of their actions.

It wasn't until a reunion night, after we'd qualified and after quite a few beers, that Johann and Kate finally decided to reveal the truth to the rest of S Group, letting the cat out of the bag about their earlier prank. We loved it! Our group erupted into hearty laughter as Johann and Kate recounted their mischievous escapade. Marveling at the duo's ability to keep the secret concealed for two years, we were delighted at their unexpected revelation.

With a mischievous glint in his eye, Johann tapped his index finger against the side of his nose, his laughter mingling with tears of amusement.

"You never know what goes on behind closed doors," he whispered to me in hushed tones, his words carrying a sense of intrigue and wonder.

He is so right; appearances can be deceiving. There's often more to people than meets the eye.

26
COMMUNITY PSYCHIATRIC TEAM

"Stop it and give yourself a chance."
Aaron T. Beck

I'd been asked to schedule bank shifts for two consecutive weeks to cover staffing shortages at the CPT office due to unexpected sickness. Fortunately, Joe willingly adjusted his work schedule, finishing early each day from Monday to Friday to take care of the children's dinner, which helped alleviate my concerns about returning home late. I was grateful to him, and I'm sure the children preferred his cooking to mine.

I arrived promptly at 8:30 am at the CPT office for duty. The CPT office was situated in a portable cabin—a hut that had been deemed 'temporary' but had been used for years. It was run down, with a leaky roof, threadbare carpet, and old-style desks.

The team at the CPT office consisted of a diverse group of highly skilled professionals, including nurses, occupational therapists, social workers, and psychiatrists. Together, they formed a multidisciplinary team with extensive experience in various fields. Their collective expertise allowed them to coordinate all aspects of community-based care, including pre- and post-hospital visits. Working collaboratively, they aimed to deliver a comprehensive and holistic support package tailored to the individual needs of each patient.

The week started with the Monday morning team meeting, which aimed to organise and coordinate tasks for the upcoming days. The team was collaborative, aiming to be non-hierarchical and inclusive. While the rest of the team focused on managing more complex clients, I was tasked with overseeing a caseload of more stable patients who required ongoing monitoring and support.

Each of the patients on my caseload required some form of assistance, including home visits, medication delivery or the administration of depot injections, mental health assessments, and simple but essential social interactions, such as a friendly chat and a cup of tea.

My role involved providing personalised care and attention to ensure that these patients received the support they needed to maintain stability and well-being in their daily lives. Each day required frequent travel between patient visits, using the hospital fleet car. I spent a sizeable portion of my time driving from one patient's home to another, ensuring timely and consistent support and care delivery.

The job underscored the importance of mobility and flexibility in providing community-based healthcare services. Despite the logistical challenges of navigating through traffic and varying distances between locations, I was able to plan each day and prioritise the well-being and comfort of my patients.

I soon got used to being on the move. Shuttling from one patient to the next, I found unexpected freedom in the time spent alone behind the wheel. As I navigated the country roads, I let loose, singing with unabashed gusto to my favourite tunes on the radio. Laughing and banging the steering wheel in time to the rhythm, I enjoyed the chance to go a bit wild on my own in the car.

Sometimes, I opted for silence, relishing the rare opportunity to think undisturbed. In those quiet moments, the rhythmic sound of the road beneath my tyres became a backdrop for introspection, and I found myself reflecting on my life and my children. Thoughts of them and their future filled my mind, prompting me to ponder the direction their lives would take. The solitude provided me with clarity and ignited a newfound sense of purpose and anticipation for the future.

I decided it was time for a change, both at home and in our routine. With renewed determination, I made plans to redecorate our living space, creating a fresh, welcoming atmosphere for my family to enjoy. I imagined an adventure holiday in the New Forest, with treetop trails, pony trekking, kayaking, and archery.

I saw four or five patients on an average day. Each encounter offered a unique glimpse into their lives, and I was fascinated by the diversity of their circumstances and surroundings. Some patients lived in compact flats nestled within towering high-rise buildings, where space was at a premium, and the hustle and bustle of urban life were constant companions. Others lived in sprawling, opulent private residences, where every corner seemed to exude luxury and comfort.

I saw a fascinating kaleidoscope of living arrangements and lifestyles. For some, their home was a sanctuary, filled with the warmth and support of a loving family. These patients were fully supported by their relatives, who offered encouragement and companionship throughout their mental health journey. Conversely, there were those who navigated their struggles alone, their homes bearing silent witness to their solitary battles. In these spaces, I saw the quiet strength of individuals facing their challenges in solitude, drawing upon their inner resilience to persevere in the face of adversity.

The state of each patient's home often seemed to mirror the intricacies of their internal worlds. Some lived amidst pristine order, their surroundings reflecting an obsessive, disciplined, and organised mindset. Others dwelled amidst chaos and clutter, their environments perhaps mirroring the turbulence within their minds.

On my rounds, I encountered a spectrum of readiness among the patients. Some greeted me with a cheerful disposition, already showered, dressed, and prepared for my visit. Their bright eyes and engaging conversation reflected a proactive approach to their mental health care. Others met me at the door in their pyjamas, their movements sluggish and their eyes clouded by the effects of medication. They grappled with the challenges of mental health, their struggles manifesting in lethargy and disengagement.

I tried to approach each interaction with compassion and empathy, offering encouragement and affirmation to those who were alert and prepared, celebrating their commitment to their well-being. For those who struggled to muster the energy, I offered gentle support and understanding, guiding them through the complexities of their mental health journey with patience and care.

Despite the stark contrasts in their living situations, I saw that they came from all walks of life and represented a broad spectrum of society. Their backgrounds, wealth, and social standing varied greatly, yet they were all united by a common thread: their struggle with mental health. Mental health knows no bounds of class, wealth, or social position. It's a great equaliser, affecting individuals from every corner of society without discrimination.

The CPT team reconvened in the familiar confines of the portacabin at the end of each day. Here, they would unwind, share insights over a cuppa, and complete their case notes. Professional discussions flowed freely as they exchanged feedback and insights, each member contributing their unique perspective. Despite the exhaustion that often accompanied their demanding work, there was a shared sense of purpose and dedication within the team. I found that my opinions were valued and respected, and I felt inspired and rejuvenated by my professional and dynamic colleagues throughout the fortnight. They were a tight-knit team, united by their commitment to their patients and each other.

As the working week ended, the CPT team had a standing tradition: they gathered at The Fyshe every Friday evening. It was their time to unwind and bond. The routine was simple yet cherished. Half the team opted for just one drink before bidding farewell and heading home to start their weekend. But for others, the allure of the bar beckoned them to linger a little longer. 'Let's have one more here before we go,' became a familiar refrain, as their laughter and lively conversation filled the air.

My Diary

What a great couple of weeks. The CPT team are a good bunch. I'm grateful I've had the chance to work with them. They've been so positive and supportive. Better than any unit I've worked at in the hospital. I wonder if there's a chance of a permanent role in the future. I've learned loads. I really enjoyed the driving and having some thinking time. Amazing to visit patients in their own homes and allowed to be autonomous. It was great to organise myself and feel free to make my own decisions about how I worked. So different from working on a ward.

27
NEW DAY – THE DAY HOSPITAL

"The function of protecting and developing health must rank even above that of restoring it when it is impaired."
Hippocrates

I'd agreed to work a full week at The Day Hospital, as Joe had taken Tom and Lizzie on holiday with his parents to Butlins. I was keen to work for the first time in this new, purpose-built establishment, designed to meet the future and evolving needs of psychiatric care in the community. I'd heard about it but, until now, hadn't had a chance to see it.

During the initial planning stages, the hospital was referred to as *The New Day Hospital*. However, as the project progressed, the name was shortened to *New Day*. The name resonated with the ethos of the facility, symbolising a fresh start and an innovative approach to mental health care. *New Day* stood for a significant step forward in the transition towards community-based mental health care, aligning with the broader movement towards deinstitutionalisation. Its modern amenities and specialist services were tailored to provide comprehensive support for individuals with mental health disorders, easing their integration into the community.

I was impressed—*New Day* exuded an atmosphere of warmth and comfort, with its clean, bright, and modern design. Gone was the sterile, clinical environment of the old day hospital. The walls were adorned with vibrant pictures of landscapes and seascapes, providing a sense of tranquillity and connection to nature. Comfortable and colourful chairs and armchairs invited patients to relax and feel at ease during their time there. The environment aimed to embrace humanity and individuality. It was a place where patients could feel safe, supported, and valued as they embarked on their journey towards mental wellness. I appreciated the innovative approach of the facility and its focus on holistic care, which encompassed not only medical treatment but also social support and rehabilitation services.

New Day provided outpatient services for individuals with mental health disorders who required structured treatment and support during the day but did not need overnight stays. The timetable offered a range of therapeutic interventions, including group therapy, art therapy, psychoeducational groups, individual counselling, medication management, occupational therapy, and social activities.

By providing intensive treatment and support during the day, *New Day* aimed to promote recovery and prevent unnecessary hospital admissions while supporting individuals to remain connected to their communities and support networks. It offered a middle ground between inpatient and outpatient care for individuals with diverse psychiatric conditions.

On admission, patients underwent a thorough assessment to determine their mental health needs, preferences, and goals. Their individual treatment plans were reviewed regularly, and patients were encouraged to actively engage in their treatment and take ownership of their mental health.

The week was enriching as I took an active part in co-facilitating various groups alongside the skilled and experienced staff. I had the opportunity to see firsthand the positive impact of group therapy and psychoeducation sessions on patients.

At the end of the week, I reflected on the meaningful interactions I'd witnessed with patients and the valuable contributions to their journey towards recovery. I felt grateful for the opportunity to experience the dynamic and compassionate team at *New Day*, bringing new opportunities for growth, learning, and connection.

On Friday, as the late afternoon sun cast long shadows through the windows, Lee, Dina, and I began tidying up and preparing to lock up the building for the weekend. The departure of the last patient marked the end of another busy week filled with therapy sessions and group activities. Together, we collected stray mugs and papers, straightened chairs, and ensured that each room was left neat and organised. As we worked, conversation flowed easily, and we discussed our plans for the weekend and reflected on the week's highlights. With all tasks completed and the building secure, we gathered our personal belongings and exchanged smiles and well wishes for the weekend ahead.

As we left through the front door, an unexpected noise caught our attention—a muffled groan coming from the nearby female toilet.

"Did you hear that?"

We exchanged questioning glances, a sense of apprehension settling over us. Lee took the initiative, stepping forward to open the main toilet door and calling out into the empty space,

"Anybody there?"

Silence.

Dina and I followed closely behind Lee.

"Hello? Is anyone there?"

Silence.

Dina, without a word, gestured towards the closed door of the middle cubicle, her expression grave. Lee knelt and peered under the door; his heart skipped a beat at what he saw. A woman lay on her side, motionless on the floor, surrounded by a pool of blood. His face showed his shock as he quickly assessed the situation.

"Claire, call for help now!" he instructed.

The door wasn't locked, and Lee pushed it open to assess the woman's condition further, carefully checking for signs of consciousness and the extent of her injuries.

"Dina, get some gloves and the grab bag," he said.

Responding swiftly, Dina rushed to retrieve the necessary supplies, while I ran to the office to dial emergency services. I relayed the details of our discovery before returning to assist my colleagues. Despite the shock of finding Christine in such a dire state, somehow, we remained composed, drawing upon our training to deal with the situation.

Christine's struggles with severe and enduring mental health issues were clear in the distressing scene before us. Her body bore the harrowing scars of years spent battling inner demons. Deep and superficial scars, old and new, crisscrossed her arms and legs, showing the history of her self-harm through cutting, burning, and scratching. Today's wound was particularly severe. A deep gash ran from wrist to elbow on her left arm, with blood still oozing gently from it. The razor blade she'd used was stuck between the thumb and index finger of her right hand, congealed with blood.

The dark, crimson blood pooled under her slashed arm and across the tiled floor, the metallic scent of iron in the air. At the edges, it appeared thicker, already coagulating into dark clots, while nearer the wound, it remained more fluid.

Lee, talking quietly to Christine, told her what he was going to do. Donning plastic gloves, he gently pressed the sides of the wound together and applied firm pressure to stem the flow. With care, Dina wrapped a bandage securely around Christine's arm. Despite her semi-conscious state, Christine groaned softly, her voice filled with remorse as she kept repeating, "Sorry, sorry."

The sound of approaching sirens heralded the arrival of the ambulance. With swift efficiency, the paramedics took over, quickly assessing Christine's condition and preparing her for transport to the hospital. Relieved, we stepped back. Despite the distressing nature of the situation, we knew Christine was now in capable hands, receiving the urgent medical attention she so needed. Psychiatric care would follow later.

I'd informed the nursing manager, the on-call duty psychiatrist, and Christine's next of kin, who were now on their way to the general hospital to support her.

Lee and Dina wasted no time attending to the cleanup, meticulously removing their gloves and disposing of them in the designated biohazard bin. They washed their hands thoroughly, ensuring any traces of blood were swiftly eradicated. I found the mop and bucket, ready to tackle the grim aftermath of the incident.

Self-harm is a complex issue, involving deliberately inflicting injury or damage to one's own body as a way of coping with emotional pain, stress, or other overwhelming feelings. It can take many forms, including cutting, burning, scratching, hitting, or pulling hair, overeating, undereating, misuse of alcohol or drugs, over exercising. Usually, cutting isn't a suicide attempt; more often, it's a way for individuals to deal with intense emotions or to feel a sense of control over their lives.

Christine's early life was complex, her childhood shaped by the chaos of alcoholism and addiction. Her parents, lost in their own struggles, were unable to provide the stability and nurturing she and her older brother desperately needed. Behind closed doors, Christine faced horrors no child should endure, scars etched upon her soul by the hands of those who should have protected her. Foster care became a transient refuge, offering brief respites from the turmoil but never truly erasing the pain she carried within. She found herself thrust into adulthood far too soon, grappling with the weight of motherhood at the tender age of fifteen. The identity of her child's father remained a mystery, rumours that the father was Christine's own brother cast a shadow that loomed over her past and present.

Her path was further complicated by an abusive marriage, a union that mirrored the dysfunction of her upbringing. Her struggles with self-harm became a silent battle, a desperate attempt to numb the pain that threatened to consume her from within. Each scar bore witness to the silent cries of a soul in turmoil, a plea for release from a darkness that threatened to engulf her. (*17)

"Well," sighed Dina, "That was an unexpected and crazy end to the week."

We all nodded in agreement. In mental health, surprises were par for the course, and each day brought its own set of challenges and uncertainties.

I chimed in with a wry smile, "That's true. I'll tell you what else is true—I'm having a glass of wine or two in the bath tonight."

"Me too," laughed Dina.

"Me three," added Lee with a chuckle.

With a shared understanding and a mutual agreement to unwind, we finished tidying up, turned off the lights, locked the door, and headed home.

With the children staying overnight at Joe's, I had the perfect opportunity to relax at home. Despite the bath and a couple of glasses of wine, my legs and back throbbed with a dull ache. My whole body felt weighed down by fatigue. With my eyelids drooping and desperate for sleep, I heaved myself upstairs to bed. Making a token effort to clean my teeth and slap on some face cream, I shuffled from the bathroom to my bed. Flopping onto it, I stretched, enjoying the welcoming hug of my mattress and duvet.

I rolled over, set the alarm clock for 8 o'clock turned off the bedside light, closed my eyes with a resigned sigh and half smile, and muttered to myself, "There we go, another day, another dollar..."

AND I COULDN'T SLEEP!

Wide awake now, unable to sleep, I wondered if Dina and Lee were alright.

I turned to write...

My Diary

It's been a good week at New Day. I've learnt a lot. It's a quality building. They seem to have really thought about the positive effect a nice environment has on people. It's a step up for mental health. The groups have been interesting. I like Lee and Dina. They all seemed to want me back, which was nice. I'll request a few more shifts.

What a Friday! I'm knackered. Now I can't sleep. What a way to finish the week! What a carry on! All that blood. Eurgh! Vile. It smelled like old tin. You never know what's going to happen next! So unexpected.

I wonder if I'll still be a nurse and working in mental health in forty years' time?

It makes me think of a line in Desiderata by Max Ehrmann: "Keep interested in your own career, however humble; it is a real possession in the changing fortunes of time." I can't imagine doing anything else... I've been frustrated, tired, fed up with the politics, but I'm never bored. Nursing has provided stability for me and the kids. Most of all, it keeps me interested.

The answer will always be YES.

28

ADDITIONAL NOTES

*1. Mental Health Nursing

The field of mental health nursing has evolved significantly over time, with notable changes and advancements occurring in various aspects of practice, education, and the overall approach to mental health care.

In the past, mental health nursing generally focused primarily on symptom management and stabilisation of patients. Today, there is a greater emphasis on a holistic approach to mental health care, which considers the individual's physical, emotional, social, and spiritual well-being. Nurses now recognise the importance of addressing the underlying causes of mental health issues and promoting overall wellness.

Mental health nursing practice was previously influenced by traditional models of care and clinical experience. Today, there is a stronger emphasis on evidence-based practice, which involves integrating the best available research evidence with clinical expertise and patient preferences. Mental health nurses now use evidence-based interventions and therapies to provide effective and individualised care to their patients.

In the 1980s and 1990s, psychotropic medications were used to manage symptoms of mental illness, often as the primary form of treatment. While medications remain an important component of mental health care, there is now a greater recognition of the need for comprehensive treatment approaches that may include therapy, lifestyle interventions, and social support. Mental health nurses play a key role in educating patients about their medications, monitoring for side effects, and promoting medication adherence.

Building therapeutic relationships with patients has always been a core aspect of mental health nursing. Now, there is a deeper understanding of the importance of empathy, active listening, and cultural competence in establishing trust and rapport with patients. Mental health nurses receive training in therapy, communication skills and cultural sensitivity to better meet the diverse needs of their patients.

Advances in technology have transformed the delivery of mental health care in recent years. Today, mental health nurses use telehealth platforms to conduct assessments, provide therapy sessions, and monitor patients remotely. Telehealth has expanded access to mental health services, becoming an integral part of mental health nursing practice in rural or underserved areas.

In recent years, there has been a growing recognition of the prevalence and impact of trauma on mental health. Mental health nursing practice is increasingly informed by trauma-informed care principles, which emphasise safety, trustworthiness, choice, collaboration, and empowerment. Mental health nurses now strive to create environments that are sensitive to the needs of individuals who have experienced trauma and promote healing and recovery.

Nurses today are equipped with a broader range of skills, knowledge, and resources to support individuals on their journey toward mental wellness and recovery.

Mental health nursing is an ever-developing discipline encompassing a wide range of skills and responsibilities aimed at providing high-quality care to patients. Experienced mental health nurses are registered nurses with specialised skills, knowledge and training. They work in a variety of healthcare settings, including hospitals, clinics, community health centres, and private practices, and may have a range of responsibilities that include conducting comprehensive mental health assessments to identify patients' needs and develop appropriate care plans, participating in the diagnosis of mental health disorders, collaborating with other healthcare providers to ensure accurate diagnosis and treatment.

Mental health nurses may administer medication and monitor patients for adverse effects or drug interactions. They may also educate patients and families on medication use, side effects, and adherence to treatment plans.

They may provide individual, group, or family therapy, using a variety of therapeutic techniques, such as cognitive-behavioural therapy, dialectical behaviour therapy, or psychodynamic therapy, to help patients manage their symptoms and improve their quality of life.

Experienced mental health nurses are trained in crisis intervention and may work in emergency departments or crisis centres to provide immediate care to patients experiencing acute mental health crises.

They also provide education to patients and their families on mental health disorders, treatment options, and community resources and support and guidance to families dealing with the challenges of caring for a loved one with mental illness.

Overall, experienced mental health nurses play a critical role in providing high-quality, compassionate care to patients with mental health disorders and promoting the overall health and well-being of their patients.

Effective mental health nursing requires the ability to establish a trusting relationship with patients, to listen to and respect their concerns, and to collaborate with them in developing treatment plans that meet their individual needs. This may involve providing education on mental health conditions and treatment options, advocating for patients' rights, and promoting their overall health and well-being.

It is important to recognise that nurses, like all healthcare providers, experience a range of emotions when caring for mental health patients. Feeling frustration, sadness, or anger at times when patients are resistant to treatment or fail to make progress is normal. However, nurses are trained to manage their emotions in a professional manner and to provide care in a non-judgmental and supportive way providing high-quality, compassionate care to their patients and promoting positive outcomes for those living with mental illness.

Evidence now supports a positive, proactive and preventative approach to mental health and wellbeing, reducing stigma.

*2. Asylum

The true meaning of asylum in terms of a mental hospital, or any other institution is a place that gives shelter and help to poor or suffering people.

St. Luke's was constructed in a manner reminiscent of numerous psychiatric hospitals from its era, positioned on a hill. This architectural choice was common for such institutions, often situated away from urban areas to provide a tranquil and secluded environment for patients. The hospital's location on high ground not only afforded panoramic views but also symbolically emphasized a sense of separation from the outside world.

This setting, with its juxtaposition of isolation and connection, speaks of the complex relationship between psychiatric institutions and the communities they serve.

Public asylums emerged in Europe and North America in the 18th and 19th centuries as a response to the increasing concern of how to manage the mentally ill. Prior to the establishment of these institutions, those suffering from mental illness were often left to fend for themselves, looked after by family, confined to prisons, or left to wander the streets as outcasts of society.

One of the earliest asylums was the Bethlehem Royal Hospital in London, founded in 1247. Commonly known as Bedlam, it initially served as a religious institution before transitioning into an asylum in the 17th century. The conditions within Bedlam were notoriously poor, with patients often subjected to inhumane treatment and neglect.

Fuelled by a growing understanding of mental illness and a desire to provide care and treatment for those affected. The institutions imposing buildings situated on the outskirts of cities or in rural areas, reflected the prevailing belief that mental illness was best treated away from the general population.

Despite the good intentions behind their creation, public asylums quickly became synonymous with overcrowding, understaffing, and appalling living conditions. Patients were often subjected to harsh and dehumanising treatments, including restraint, isolation, and even physical abuse. The asylum system was also used as a means of social control, with individuals deemed 'undesirable' or 'deviant' confined against their will.

The late 19th and early 20th centuries saw a shift in attitudes towards mental illness, driven in part by advancements in medical knowledge and changing social opinion. Advocates for change campaigned for reform, calling attention to the inhumane conditions within asylums and advocating for more compassionate and humane treatment.

This reform movement led to significant changes in the way mental illness was perceived and treated. Public asylums began to adopt more humane and patient-centred approaches to care, focusing on rehabilitation and recovery rather than confinement and control. The rise of psychotherapy and psychiatric medications further revolutionised the treatment of mental illness, allowing many individuals to live more fulfilling and productive lives out of institutional settings.

By the onset of the 20th century, the escalating number of admissions led to significant overcrowding in public asylums. Financial resources were often slashed during periods of economic downturn. During the 1920s and 1930s, the first suggestions for community-based alternatives emerged and were cautiously put into practice, although asylum populations continued to rise until the 1950s. The deinstitutionalisation movement gained prominence in various Western nations during the 1950s and 1960s. The arguments presented to the public, as well as the timing and pace of reforms, varied from country to country. Sociologists and other advocates argued that these institutions fostered dependency, passivity, exclusion, and disability, leading individuals to become institutionalised.

Some argued that community services would be more cost-effective, with the advent of new psychiatric medications making it more viable to reintegrate individuals into society. However, there were divergent perspectives on deinstitutionalisation among mental health professionals, public officials, families, advocacy groups, citizens, and unions.

During the 1990s in the UK, a significant shift occurred in the approach to mental health care, marked by a transition away from traditional psychiatric hospitals towards community-based services, aiming to provide individuals with mental health issues greater autonomy, support, and integration into society.

The decision to move away from psychiatric hospitals stemmed from a growing recognition of the limitations and shortcomings of institutional care. These hospitals, often characterised by overcrowding, substandard conditions, and a lack of personalised treatment, were seen as isolating and stigmatising environments that hindered individuals' recovery and well-being.

Advocates for deinstitutionalisation argued that community-based services could offer more personalised, holistic, and humane care. They believed that by providing support within the community, individuals with mental health issues could lead more fulfilling and independent lives while maintaining connections with family, friends, and society at large.

Throughout the 1990s, the UK government implemented various policies and initiatives to support the shift towards community-based mental health care. This included investing in community mental health teams, crisis intervention services, supported housing, and day centres. These services aimed to provide a range of support options tailored to individuals' needs, promoting recovery, social inclusion, and increasing quality of life.

Advances in psychiatric medication and therapeutic interventions facilitated the transition to community-based care by offering effective treatment options that could be administered in non-hospital settings. This helped to alleviate some of the concerns about the feasibility of managing mental health issues in the community.

The move towards community-based care was not without its challenges. Critics raised concerns about the availability and adequacy of community services, as well as issues related to funding, staffing, and coordination between different agencies and organisations involved in mental health care delivery.

Despite these challenges, the 1990s marked a significant turning point in mental health care in the UK, with the emphasis shifting towards empowering individuals with mental health issues to live meaningful and fulfilling lives within their communities. This transition laid the groundwork for ongoing efforts to promote mental health and well-being, reduce stigma, and ensure that individuals receive the support and care they need to thrive.

St. Luke's underwent a transformation over a three-year period where patients were relocated from the hospital to homes in the community. While this change may have been positive for some individuals, offering them a new environment and possibly more independence, others found it difficult to adjust, missing the familiarity, support, and sense of belonging they experienced at St Luke's.

The patients longed for the return of their social club and hospital shop. Many of them had found purposeful employment within the hospital, contributing by assisting in the laundry, tending to the gardens, or delivering mail to various wards and departments. With the transition from hospital to community living, many lost their sense of belonging, meaning and purpose.

The transition also impacted on staff, who had formed close bonds with the patients and felt a sense of loss or displacement with the closure of the hospital.

Now, like many similar institutions, St. Luke's is a housing complex, with its wards repurposed and converted into apartments and flats. There is a communal gym, swimming pool and café. This repurposing reflects a shift in the use of the space, from providing medical care to offering residential accommodation. It is a common phenomenon in many places where these old institutions have been adapted to meet the changing needs in society.

*3. The Back-Office

The designation of the Nursing Office as 'the back-office' despite its location on the second floor at the front of the hospital at first glance seemed odd.

In many hospitals, the term 'back-office' is not necessarily indicative of its physical placement but rather denotes the administrative hub where essential functions such as scheduling, staffing, and record-keeping are centralised. This administrative centre served as the nerve centre of the hospital's operations, facilitating communication and coordination among various departments and personnel.

The historical evolution of hospital terminology often plays a role in shaping perceptions and naming conventions. Over time, certain designations become ingrained in the institutional culture, reflecting the unique ethos and traditions of the healthcare setting.

The Nursing Office, being referred to as 'the back-office,' reflects a longstanding tradition or colloquialism within hospital communities. A quirk of language that added character to the institution while serving as a point of familiarity for staff and visitors alike.

*4. The Midnight Returns

The Midnight Returns document served as a vital record of daily ward activity within the hospital, capturing a snapshot of the ever-changing landscape of patient care and management. Handwritten with meticulous detail, it provided a succinct yet comprehensive summary of the events unfolding within the wards every twelve hours.

At its core, the document functioned as a conduit of communication, bridging the gap between shifts, and ensuring continuity of care for patients under the hospital's watchful eye. Within its pages, the nuances of patient interactions and medical interventions were dutifully recorded.

Among its contents were documented any issues or concerns pertaining to patient care, providing a platform for caregivers to communicate vital information and address emerging challenges in real-time to senior managers.

Furthermore, it served as a repository of logistical information, documenting the comings and goings of patients within the hospital's wards. Recording patient outings, documenting admissions and discharges, or noting the unfortunate passing of a patient, every event was documented.

In addition, the document acted as a barometer of bed occupancy, providing valuable insights into the ebb and flow of patient admissions and discharges within each ward. This critical information enabled hospital administrators to allocate resources efficiently, to ensure that patient needs were met in a timely and effective manner.

The process of completing the document in duplicate, using navy-blue carbon paper, emphasised the hospital's commitment to record-keeping and accountability. Each entry made on the original document was duplicated, ensuring that vital information was preserved and accessible to key stakeholders throughout the hospital.

Each ward and department diligently filled out individual Ward Returns documents. With handwritten entries, the carbon paper facilitated the creation of an exact replica of each page. This duplication process was instrumental in mitigating the risk of data loss or misplacement, providing an additional layer of security to the hospital's record-keeping practices.

Once completed, one copy of the Ward Returns document remained on the ward, filed, and serving as a tangible record of the day's activities and patient interactions. Accessible to frontline staff and caregivers, this filed copy provided a valuable reference point for ongoing patient care and decision-making, ensuring that all members of the healthcare team were informed and aligned in their approach.

Simultaneously, the duplicate copy of the Ward Returns document was filed in the back-office, where it served as a central repository of information for hospital administrators, supervisors, and support staff. This centralised filing system facilitated efficient data management and retrieval, empowering hospital leadership to track trends, analyse patterns, and make informed decisions regarding resource allocation and operational planning.

The use of carbon paper ensured that each duplicate copy was legible and durable, standing the test of time amidst the rigors of daily hospital operations. Whether consulted for routine updates or referenced in moments of crisis, in essence, the Returns document served as a trusted source of information, to guide the hospital's collective efforts in delivering compassionate and effective patient care.

The Midnight Returns, with its grandiose name befitting its importance, offered a comprehensive overview of the bed state for the entire hospital, amalgamating and capturing patient admissions, discharges, and transfers throughout the day. Compiled with the aid of carbon paper, this document stood as evidence of the hospital's commitment to thoroughness and accountability.

The process of compiling the - 'Midnight Returns' -, was overseen by the Night Matron or Nursing Officer and served as a pivotal moment in the nightly operations of the hospital. As the witching hour approached and the bustle of the day gave way to the quietude of night, these dedicated individuals assumed the responsibility of amalgamating data from each Ward Return onto a master sheet; a process steeped in tradition and precision.

With each stroke of the pen, the Night Matron or Nursing Officer documented bed occupancy, patient demographics, and any notable incidents or concerns seen throughout the day.

This multi-layered approach ensured that vital information was preserved and accessible to key stakeholders, from senior managers to frontline staff, in the event of unforeseen circumstances or emergencies.

Once completed, the Midnight Returns served as a cornerstone of the handover process, offering invaluable insights into the hospital's operations and patient care initiatives. Each Ward Returns sheet, annotated with the date of its creation, was filed, together with the Midnight Returns in a red ring-bound folder, symbolising its importance as a historical record of hospital life, each folder labelled and dated: JAN – DEC (year) MIDNIGHT RETURNS.

The folders lined the bookshelves of the back-office like silent sentinels, bearing witness to the myriad interactions and interventions that defined the institution's commitment to patient care.

For five years, these files stood as testaments to the dedication and diligence of the hospital staff. When storage space became scarce, files that had served their purpose in the daily operations of the nursing office were destined for a new chapter in their journey and moved to attics and storerooms of the hospital.

Though relegated to the recesses of memory, the archived files remained guardians of the hospital's legacy amidst the dust and shadows.

*5. The Nursing Handover

The nursing handover represents a pivotal moment in the continuum of patient care, embodying the essence of seamless communication and collaboration within healthcare settings. At its core, a nursing handover constitutes the transfer of responsibility and vital information pertaining to a patient's care from one nurse or shift to another.

At the end of each shift, a nursing handover serves as a crucial juncture where pertinent details regarding each patient's condition, treatment plan, medications, and any notable changes or concerns. This information is hopefully relayed with precision and clarity. This exchange of information ensures continuity of care and fosters a shared understanding among nursing staff, thereby safeguarding the well-being and safety of patients under their charge.

One of the first tasks undertaken by the receiving team is to verify that all patients are accounted for. Through cross-referencing of patient records and completing a walkthrough of the ward, the team ensures that no individual had been overlooked or misplaced during the transition between shifts. This step is crucial for maintaining patient safety and continuity of care.

Following the patient accountability check, the receiving team plans the roles and responsibilities of each staff member for the duration of the shift. Drawing upon their collective expertise and familiarity with the ward's operations, tasks and assignments are allocated based on the unique needs of the patients. This proactive approach enables the team to optimise workflow and prioritise patient care initiatives.

The receiving team facilitates a physical handover of the ward keys for the medication trolley and controlled drugs cupboard. This exchange of keys symbolises a transfer of responsibility and accountability to ensure that access to essential medications and supplies remains secure and tightly regulated throughout the shift.

Effective handovers are essential to ensure continuity of care for patients and to prevent errors or lapses in care. The reports must be accurate and communicated with colleagues to ensure that all necessary information is shared.

To an outsider, the abbreviations used in nursing handovers is like listening to a foreign language. It is important to note that clear communication is essential to ensure patient safety, and the use of abbreviations should be limited to those that are widely recognised and understood by all healthcare professionals involved in the handover.

Some of the common abbreviations used are ADL: Activities of Daily Living, BP: Blood Pressure, C/O: Complains Of, C&S: Culture and Sensitivity, D/C: Discharge, IV: Intravenous, PRN: As needed, QID: Four times a day, SOB: Shortness of Breath, TID: Three times a day, WNL: Within Normal Limits.

*6. Uniforms

Uniforms at St Luke's were meticulously colour-coded according to staff grade, serving as a visual indicator of rank and responsibility. Male staff members adhered to a standard timeless attire consisting of black hospital-issue trousers, a crisp white shirt with coloured epaulettes, and a clip-on black tie.

Each staff member was issued with a set of five uniforms, collected from the sewing room, where name tags had been sewn into each item. Dresses, shirts, trousers, epaulettes, even ties received a name tag.

For G-grade ward Sisters, navy cotton blue nurses' uniforms with a belted buckle represented the hallmark of their authority and expertise, distinguishing them as leaders within the nursing hierarchy.

Meanwhile, F-grade and E-grade Senior Staff Nurses and Staff Nurses donned fine checked polyester blue and white dresses, reflecting their roles as caregivers and advocates for patient well-being.

D-grade Enrolled Nurses were identified by their fine checked polyester green and white dresses, signifying their dedication to providing skilled nursing care under the guidance of their superiors.

A, B, and C-grade nursing assistants, entrusted with a range of supportive tasks, wore fine checked polyester beige and white dresses; a subtle yet distinct uniform that accentuated their integral role within the healthcare team.

Irrespective of their rank or role, all staff members were issued a clip-on identity badge and a set of hospital keys. These badges and keys served as tangible reminders of their collective responsibility to ensure the welfare and security of patients and colleagues alike.

The strict policy against wearing hospital uniforms away from the hospital premises was rooted in infection control protocols, aimed at minimising the risk of cross-contamination and safeguarding public health.

Violating this policy carried serious repercussions, including disciplinary action that could potentially jeopardise one's employment status.

Despite the clear directives and potential consequences, occasional instances arose where individuals, driven by urgency or oversight, opted to take the risk and wear their uniforms in the community. In these instances, the temptation to expedite errands or fulfil personal obligations often outweighed adherence to established protocols.

Often, those who took this chance managed to evade detection, their actions going unnoticed amidst the hustle and bustle of everyday life.

Individuals caught wearing their uniforms outside the hospital were swiftly summoned before the authorities to face the consequences of their actions. First-time offenders received a verbal warning as a stern reminder of the seriousness of their breach in protocol and the potential consequences for patient safety.

Repeat offenders, however, faced escalating disciplinary measures, including written warnings that documented the severity of their infractions. Persistent disregard for the uniform policy ultimately culminated in the possibility of dismissal, signalling a definitive end to their employment within the hospital.

The decision to wear mufti on acute wards varies depending on the policies of individual hospitals or healthcare organizations, as well as the specific needs and preferences of staff and patients.

The rationale at St Luke's was that wearing mufti provided greater comfort and flexibility, allowing staff to move more easily and perform their duties more effectively. Patients can sometimes feel threatened and become agitated or violent when they see staff members in uniforms. By wearing ordinary clothes, staff can appear less threatening and avoid escalating any already tense situations. Wearing normal clothes can help to break down barriers and staff appear more approachable, fostering a sense of equality and partnership between staff and patients which helps to develop a better therapeutic alliance.

*7. The Toilet Round

The toilet round involved taking all the patients to the toilet whether they wanted to go or not. Whether they knew where they were going or not, they were all taken to the toilets and 'toileted'. Those who needed wheelchairs and the help of two staff went first. Those who could walk unaided followed behind with lots of encouragement.

The 'toilet round' represented a fundamental aspect of patient care and hygiene within the hospital, ensuring that everyone's needs were met as far as possible with dignity and compassion. Scheduled both before and after supper, this routine encompassed a systematic approach to assisting patients with toileting, regardless of their preferences or abilities.

The process was conducted while acknowledging each patient's unique circumstances and ensuring their comfort and well-being throughout.

Following supper, the 'toilet round' resumed, reaffirming the commitment to maintaining patient hygiene and comfort as an integral component of holistic care. Patients, whether they could walk unaided or required assistance, were guided once more to the toilet facilities, accompanied by supportive staff members who offered encouragement and reassurance on the way.

In the rhythm of the 'toilet round,' continued at set times, day in, day out. Patients' needs were attended to physically but also emotionally as they chatted with staff, fostering an environment of trust and respect at an intimate and necessary time.

The nursing notes were referred to as the Kardex, meticulous documentation of bowel movements was a critical aspect of patient care. Various abbreviations were employed to succinctly capture the nature and frequency of bowel movements, ensuring clarity and consistency in recording practices. Some of the abbreviations used included:

B.O: Bowels open. Indicates the patient has had a bowel movement.

BWO: Bowels wide open. Indicates the patient has experienced significant bowel movements.

SBO: Small bowels open. Indicates a bowel movement of smaller volume.

LBO: Loose bowels open. Indicates a bowel movement of loose or watery in consistency.

App. const: Appears constipated - suggesting that the patient may be experiencing symptoms suggestive of constipation, such as infrequent or difficult bowel movements.

Using standardised abbreviations in the Kardex, nurses could efficiently communicate key information about bowel movements, facilitating comprehensive assessments, interventions, and follow-up care. This systematic approach not only ensured the continuity of care but also empowered healthcare providers to respond promptly to changes in the patient's condition, optimising outcomes and promoting overall well-being.

Recording bowel movements may seem trivial to those not involved in caregiving roles, but for nurses, it constitutes a vital aspect of patient care and health monitoring. Bowel habits serve as a window into an individual's overall health, reflecting dietary intake, hydration levels, and the efficiency of the digestive system.

Meticulous documentation and observation of bowel movements enable the detection of subtle changes that may indicate underlying health concerns. Changes in stool consistency, colour, frequency, or the presence of blood can provide valuable insights into gastrointestinal health and functioning. They can indicate whether a patient is consuming enough fibre and fluids, or if their digestive system is experiencing disruptions such as slow or rapid transit times.

Persistent alterations in bowel habits when accompanied by symptoms like abdominal pain, bloating, or weight loss, may signify underlying medical conditions such as bowel cancer or inflammatory bowel disease. Early detection and intervention can greatly improve treatment outcomes and overall prognosis.

Constipation can lead to a host of discomforts and complications, including stomach problems, cramps, bloating, nausea, and loss of appetite. In severe cases, it may even cause extreme confusion, posing significant risks to the patient's well-being.

*8. Hospital Food

The mea's they produced were simple and basic, but served to nourish and sustain patients, prioritising essential nutritional requirements over culinary extravagance. The menu was standardised to accommodate the diverse dietary needs of patients, each dish, thoughtfully crafted and prepared.

From hearty stews and comforting casseroles to nourishing soups and wholesome salads, the menu reflected a balanced approach to meeting patients' nutritional needs while adhering to budgetary constraints and logistical considerations.

While the culinary offerings may not have rivalled those of haute cuisine establishments, they fulfilled a vital role in the healing process, providing sustenance and comfort to patients during their stay. With dedication the kitchen staff transformed humble ingredients into meals that nourished both body and spirit.

Breakfast at the hospital followed a comforting and familiar routine, offering patients a selection of wholesome options to start their day. Porridge, a timeless classic renowned for its hearty and warming qualities, took centre stage alongside a variety of cereals and toast.

There was an array of toppings, including butter, jams, marmalade, Marmite, Bovril, and peanut butter, to appeal to a range of palates and dietary preferences.

Occasionally, the breakfast menu featured tinned grapefruit, adding a refreshing and tangy touch to the meal.

In its simplicity and familiarity, breakfast at the hospital was a comforting ritual amidst the routine of hospital life.

Lunchtime brought forth a comforting array of cooked meals with hearty flavours and familiar favourites. Among the offerings were classic dishes such as shepherd's pie, a savoury mixture of minced meat, vegetables, and creamy mashed potato topping, and cheese and potato pie, a rich and satisfying alternative.

For those craving seafood, there was baked fish. Minced chicken, sausages, braised beef, and casseroled pork offered a variety of protein-rich options to suit different tastes and dietary preferences. Each dish was paired with creamy mashed potatoes or plain boiled rice and a medley of boiled vegetables carrots, peas, sweetcorn, and cabbage.

A large jug of thick, light brown gravy was available at every meal.

Patients were treated to dessert choices ranging from classic sponge and custard, or the refreshing simplicity of jelly and ice cream.

The lunchtime spread at the hospital aimed to be wholesome and satisfying, with familiar flavours that brought a sense of warmth and reassurance to patients during their stay.

Supper time brought forth a further array of foodstuffs.

At weekends, the menu featured a hearty bowl of soup accompanied by slices of freshly baked bread and butter, along with a selection of sandwiches filled with ham, cheese, or egg. The meal ended on a sweet note, with slices of cake or individual cupcakes and biscuits to round off the teatime experience.

During the week, the offerings remained equally inviting but repetitive, with a slight variation in choices. Patients could indulge in a selection of sandwiches, filled with ham, cheese, or egg or opt for heartier fare such as scrambled eggs, beans, or sausages served alongside tinned tomatoes and toast.

Throughout the week, the suppertime menu served as a reassuring constant, offering patients respite and nourishment amidst the routines of hospital life.

For patients requiring assistance with feeding or those at risk of choking, specialised care and supervision were paramount to ensure their safety and well-being during mealtimes. These individuals were grouped together under the attentive watch of two nurses.

Their diet was tailored to meet their specific needs and consisted of minced, mashed, squashed, pureed, and soft foods, prepared to ensure ease of swallowing and digestion. The resulting dishes often bore an indeterminate hue of beige and white, their appearance secondary to their texture and suitability for consumption.

From pureed vegetables to soft grains and tender meats, every component of the diet underwent careful preparation to ensure that it met the unique needs of the individuals it served.

*9. Shift work

Working shifts can bring about a range of emotions and experiences. Some people find it difficult to adjust to changing shift patterns and can become isolated or lonely due to the lack of social interaction. On night shift, it can be difficult to sleep in the day. Staff who are physically exhausted struggle to keep a healthy eating and sleep schedule. Additionally, the body's natural circadian rhythms may be disrupted, leading to mood swings, irritability, and difficulty concentrating. Some staff describe hallucinating and a strange sickly sensation that feels like boat rock.

Isolation and loneliness is a common experience among night shift workers, as social interactions are limited, and maintaining connections with friends and family may be more challenging. The inability to sleep well during the day due to factors such as noise, light, or household responsibilities can contribute to feelings of fatigue and exhaustion.

Physical symptoms such as fatigue, difficulty concentrating, and irritability are also common among night shift workers and can affect job performance and overall well-being. The body's internal clock, which regulates various physiological processes, may struggle to adjust to the demands of working during nighttime hours, leading to mood swings and difficulty focusing.

Hallucinations and sensations like feeling as if on a rocking boat are extreme manifestations of the body's struggle to adapt to the night shift schedule. These experiences may be related to sleep deprivation, circadian rhythm disruption, or other factors associated with working overnight hours.

The night hours can also present unique challenges, such as increased responsibility and less support from management or colleagues. Workers on the night shift may experience a heightened sense of pressure to perform well without the same level of resources available during the day. The lack of natural light and exposure to sunlight can also contribute to feelings of lethargy and depression.

Despite these challenges, some staff found that working the night shift suited their lifestyle and preferences, tending to either love it, or loathe it.

*10. Observation levels

Observations, abbreviated as 'Obs' or checks, constitute a critical aspect of the routine on every acute ward. In such settings, patients are regularly assessed based on their risk level to themselves or others. This assessment leads to the assignment of an observation level, which determines the frequency and intensity of checks required, all of which should be documented.

On Maple Ward, the observation levels ranged from 1 to 4, each corresponding to different degrees of risk or need for monitoring. These levels likely dictated how often patients were observed, the level of supervision they received, and the precautions taken to ensure their safety and well-being during their stay on the ward.

Such systematic monitoring is essential for providing appropriate care and intervention when necessary, helping to maintain a safe and supportive environment for all patients under their care.

Level 1 meant that the patient needed to always remain in arm's length of the nurse. This was for patients with an elevated level of risk or suicide. One nurse was assigned every hour to always stay with the patient.

Level 2 meant that the patient needed to be checked on every 15 minutes.

Level 3 meant that the patient needed to be checked on every 30 minutes.

Level 4 meant that the patient was subject to the standard hourly checks for the ward during the day.

*11. Psychosis

Grief and sleep deprivation can be a contributing factor to the development of psychosis. When people are deprived of sleep for prolonged periods, it can cause changes in brain chemistry, such as a decrease in the levels of dopamine, which can lead to the onset of psychotic symptoms.

Studies show that sleep deprivation can lead to hallucinations, delusions, and other symptoms of psychosis. Lack of sleep can also make it more difficult for individuals to regulate their emotions and respond appropriately to stressful situations, which can exacerbate psychotic symptoms.

Psychosis can be caused by a range of factors, including genetic, environmental, and neurological factors. It is important to note that psychosis is a complex condition and the causes of it can vary widely from person to person.

There are different classes of medications used to treat psychosis, including antipsychotics, mood stabilisers, and antidepressants. The specific medication prescribed depends on the individual's symptoms, medical history, and other factors.

Antipsychotic medications are often the first-line treatment for psychosis. These drugs work by blocking the activity of dopamine, a neurotransmitter that is believed to be involved in the development of psychotic symptoms.

Mood stabilizers such as lithium and valproate can also be used to manage psychotic symptoms in individuals with bipolar disorder.

Antidepressants may also be prescribed for individuals with co-occurring depression or anxiety, which can worsen psychotic symptoms.

While medications can be effective in managing psychotic symptoms, they may also have side effects. These can include weight gain, sedation, dry mouth, and movement disorders. It is important for individuals taking these medications to be closely monitored by their healthcare provider to ensure that the benefits of the medication outweigh the potential risks.

*12. Suicide

Suicide is a deeply complex and tragic phenomenon that has a profound impact on individuals, families, and communities. It is a manifestation of extreme emotional distress, often stemming from a combination of factors such as mental illness, trauma, social isolation, and adverse life circumstances.

Despite its prevalence, suicide is still surrounded by stigma and misunderstanding, hindering open dialogue and effective prevention efforts. Each suicide stands for not only a life lost but also a ripple effect of pain and grief that extends far beyond the individual.

Addressing suicide requires a multifaceted approach that encompasses mental health awareness, access to quality care, social support systems, and efforts to address underlying risk factors. It is imperative to foster empathy, understanding, and proactive intervention to prevent future tragedies and promote mental well-being for all.

Predicting suicide is incredibly challenging and fraught with ethical considerations. Suicide risk assessment is a complex process that involves evaluating numerous factors such as mental health history, current psychological state, social support network, past suicide attempts, and environmental stressors. Certain risk factors may increase the likelihood of suicide, but they do not provide a definitive prediction of an individual's actions.

Hindsight offers a unique perspective, often revealing details or patterns that were not apparent at the time. In the context of suicide, hindsight can lead to feelings of guilt, regret, or a sense of missed opportunities to intervene. Individuals, including both staff and loved ones, may find themselves questioning whether they could have done more to prevent the tragedy.

It is important to recognise that responsibility for suicide is complex and multifaceted. Hindsight may shed light on warning signs or risk factors that were missed, it's essential to approach these reflections with compassion and understanding.

Responsibility for suicide cannot be placed solely on any one individual or factor. Instead, it requires a comprehensive understanding of the interplay between biological, psychological, social, and environmental factors that contribute to suicidal behaviour.

By working together and learning from past experiences, we can strive to create a world where individuals feel valued, supported, and empowered to seek help when struggling with suicidal thoughts.

*13. Windrush nurses

In the late 1940s, there were 54,000 nursing vacancies, so the Ministries of Health and Labour, the Colonial Office, the Royal College of Nursing, and the General Nursing Council worked together to recruit Caribbean women to fill the nurse shortage in Britain.

The nurses who came to the United Kingdom at this time are part of what's known as the Windrush Generation: approximately half a million people who migrated from Caribbean countries to the UK between 1948 and 1971, in response to the British government's call for labour to help rebuild the country after World War II.

Trainee nurses were drawn from all over the world, but the majority were recruited from the Caribbean Islands. By 1977, overseas employees occupied 12% of all student nurses and midwife roles, with over two thirds from the Caribbean.

Windrush nurses often weren't given the option to choose which field of nursing to work in. They were pushed to work for marginalised groups such as the chronically sick, elderly people, people with disabilities, and the increasing number of people with post-war trauma in psychiatric hospitals, and often denied nursing in any other area that would help them progress in their career.

*14. Not all carers care

People are drawn to the medical professions for a variety of reasons, often stemming from a combination of personal, altruistic, intellectual, and practical motivations. Many are inherently compassionate and have a strong desire to help alleviate suffering and improve the well-being of others. Medicine is a field that requires critical thinking, problem-solving skills, and a lifelong commitment to learning. For individuals who enjoy intellectual challenges and continuous learning, the medical profession can offer a stimulating environment where they can apply scientific knowledge to solve complex problems and make important decisions.

Working in medicine often provides a keen sense of purpose and fulfilment for some people. Healthcare professionals can contribute to the greater good and make meaningful contributions to society by promoting health, preventing disease, and treating illness.

Some individuals are drawn to medicine because of firsthand experiences with illness, injury, or healthcare providers. They may have been inspired by the care they received or witnessed the impact that healthcare professionals can have on patients and families during challenging times.

While financial considerations are not always the primary motivation for choosing a career in medicine, the potential for financial stability and a comfortable income can be appealing to many individuals, especially considering the significant investment of time and resources required to complete medical education and training.

Overall, the diverse and multifaceted nature of the medical professions attracts individuals from various backgrounds who share a common commitment to improving the health and well-being of individuals and communities.

There is a small percentage of people who work in health because of the power and control it gives them. Power and control in healthcare are complex concepts that can manifest in numerous ways within the system.

Doctors, nurses, psychiatrists, or other care providers typically hold a significant amount of power and authority in their interactions with patients. This power dynamic can influence the decisions made regarding diagnosis, treatment options, and care plans.

Patients may feel vulnerable and reliant on the expertise and guidance of their healthcare providers, which can affect their ability to advocate for themselves and make informed decisions about their healthcare.

Unfortunately, instances of professionals abusing their positions of power and trust do occur in healthcare, as they can in any field where there is a power dynamic between provider and recipient. Such cases are relatively rare compared to the vast number of healthcare professionals who serve their patients with care and integrity, but any instance of abuse or misconduct is concerning and must be addressed appropriately. Medical negligence cases occur when healthcare providers fail to meet the standard of care expected in their profession, resulting in harm to patients. Negligence can stem from errors in diagnosis, treatment, medication administration, or surgical procedures.

Some healthcare professionals may exploit their positions of authority to take advantage of vulnerable patients. This can include financial exploitation, sexual misconduct, or other forms of abuse.

*15. Electroconvulsive therapy

ECT, or electroconvulsive therapy, has a history of being a controversial treatment method in psychiatry.

At St Luke's and other psychiatric institutions in the 70s, 80s and 90s, ECT was used regularly as an intervention for major depressive disorder, severe cases of depression, bipolar disorder, mania, catatonia and sometimes schizophrenia particularly when other treatments had proven ineffective, or the patient's condition was deemed life-threatening.

For many patients, a course of ECT consisted of multiple sessions spread out over several weeks. The exact number of treatments varied but tended to involve anywhere from 6 to 12 sessions, with some patients requiring more or fewer treatments based on their individual needs.

In the 1990s, the use of ECT in the UK was regulated and governed by guidelines set by professional bodies like the Royal College of Psychiatrists and the Mental Health Act.

The use of ECT has changed over time due to advances in psychiatric treatment options, evolving medical practices, and shifts in societal attitudes towards mental health care. Specific data on the exact reduction in ECT usage from the 1990s to today varies depending on region and healthcare practices but there has been a general decline in its use as a primary treatment for mental health conditions since the 1990s.

The decline is partly attributed to the development and increased availability of alternative treatments, including new medications, psychotherapies, and brain stimulation techniques. Healthcare providers are required to ensure that patients fully understand the potential risks and benefits of ECT before consenting to treatment. This focus on patient autonomy has likely contributed to a more cautious approach to the use of ECT.

Efforts to reduce stigma surrounding mental illness and its treatments may also have contributed to decreased reliance on ECT. With increased public awareness and acceptance of mental health issues, individuals are more proactive and inclined to seek and receive a wider range of treatments.

*16. Nightingale and Cavell

Edith Cavell was a British nurse, remembered for her bravery during World War I. She helped save the lives of soldiers from both sides without discrimination, and she was eventually executed by the Germans for her role in assisting Allied soldiers to escape German-occupied Belgium.

Florence Nightingale gained prominence during the Crimean War and is often considered the founder of modern nursing. She and her team of nurses improved sanitary conditions in military hospitals, reducing the mortality rate by introducing better hygiene practices. Nightingale's contributions to nursing laid the foundation for modern nursing education and practice.

*17. Self-Harm

While self-harm is clearly not a healthy or effective way to cope with emotional pain, but it is important to recognise that for some people, it is their only way to cope. It may provide temporary relief; it can also lead to long term chronic physical and psychological consequences.

Self-harm is often stigmatised and misunderstood, often viewed as attention-seeking behaviour, or dismissed as a sign of weakness or mental instability. Those who engage in self-harm often face harsh judgment and condemnation rather than compassionate support.

Over the decades, with increased awareness and education about mental health issues, open discussions and greater empathy and understanding, there has been a gradual but significant shift in attitudes to self-harm.

There is a growing recognition that self-harm is often a coping mechanism used by individuals to deal with overwhelming emotions or trauma. It is understood as a complex issue with underlying psychological factors that require sensitive and compassionate support. Mental health professionals, as well as broader society, acknowledge the importance of providing non-judgmental support and access to proper resources for those who struggle with self-harm.

Efforts to promote mental health awareness and destigmatise self-harm have led to the development of specialised interventions and support services tailored to individuals who self-harm. These include therapy, support groups, crisis hotlines, and online resources, all aimed at providing guidance, understanding, and help to those in need.

In addition, there has been a shift towards empowering individuals who self-harm to seek help and engage in recovery without fear of judgment, creating a more inclusive and supportive environment for all individuals, regardless of their struggles.

Acknowledgements

Thank you always to my rock Keith, Mathew and Stephanie. I am blessed with the love and support of family and good friends. Special thanks to Carol, Tracey, John and Jocelyne for giving me the feedback and encouragement I needed to write this book.
I've worked with many inspirational staff and patients over the years, and I've included lots of them in these stories. My career has been challenging at times, but for the most part, people are resilient and the privilege of sharing their stories and lives, meeting their families and being a part of their recovery has been hugely rewarding.

Mental health is everybody's business.

Printed in Great Britain
by Amazon